SPIDER'S VOICE

Gloria Skurzynski

SPIDER'S VOICE

Aladdin Paperbacks

New York London Toronto Sydney Singapore

First Aladdin Paperbacks edition April 2001
Text copyright © 1999 by Gloria Skurzynski

Aladdin Paperbacks
An imprint of Simon & Schuster
Children's Publishing Division
1230 Avenue of the Americas
New York, NY 10020

Designed by Lisa Vega
The text for this book was set in Cochin.

Printed and bound in the United States of America.
2 4 6 8 10 9 7 5 3 1

The Library of Congress has cataloged the hardcover edition as follows:
Skurzynski, Gloria.
Spider's voice / by Gloria Skurzynski. — 1st ed. p. cm.
Summary: Because he is a young mute person who can hear, Aran
becomes involved in the adventures of Eloise and Abelard, France's
most famous lovers, who lived during the twelfth century.
ISBN: 0-689-82149-2 (hc.)
1. Abelard, Peter, 1079-142 — Juvenile fiction. 2. Héloïse, 1101-1164 —
Juvenile fiction. 3. France — History — Medieval period, 987-1515 —
Juvenile fiction. [1. Abelard, Peter, 1079-1142 — Fiction. 2. Héloïse,
1101-1164 — Fiction 3. France — History — Medieval period, 987-1515 —
Fiction. 4. Mute persons — Fiction. 5. Physically handicapped — Fiction.]
I. Title.   PZ7.S6287Sp 1999   [Fic] — dc21   98-7981

ISBN: 0-689-84208-2 (Aladdin pbk.)

For Ed, for half a century and forever

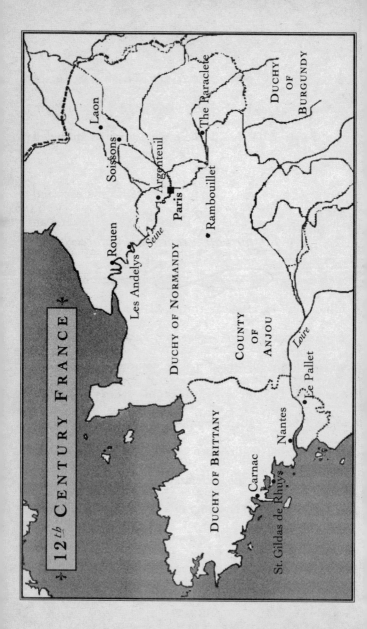

I HAVE ALWAYS BEEN ABLE TO SPEAK INSIDE MY HEAD, but not with my tongue. As a tiny child, I would try to say words. All I could make were terrible strangled noises.

My father would then strike me on the ears and shout to my mother, "An idiot! You've given me an idiot!" Her eyes darkening with fear, my mother would shake her head and clasp me against her. If my father was as cruel as the devil—and he was—my mother was an angel. Near her, I would try to talk, softly, almost silently. But even with her kind encouragement, I could never make the words come out right. After she died, I stopped making any sounds at all, until that night when Abelard, the great orator, came at me with his knife and slashed . . .

But wait! I'm spinning this tale without a pattern. Let me go back to the beginning, to the center of the web that holds me.

CHAPTER ONE

THEY CHRISTENED ME ARAN, if I was ever actually christened—I'm not sure.

Certainly my father had nothing with which to pay a priest for a christening. We were lucky if we had enough to eat. My father and my older brother managed to shovel enough food into their greedy mouths to stay strong—it was my mother and I who nearly starved. I think that is the reason I was so small.

My first memories are of my mother spinning. Still a baby, I would lie on the dirt floor of our hut, nestled on bundles of wool shorn from my father's sheep. Above my head, hanging from a perfect, thin thread, a spindle constantly whirled, growing fatter by the hour as my mother fed it fleece from the distaff she held beneath her arm. In early spring, when the sheep were first shorn and the days were still cold, I had a thick pile of wool to lie on. By summer, when even the nights had become warm, the wool would be gone, spun into delicate yarn by my mother's swift, clever, worn fingers.

My mother talked to me all the time; in fact, I was the only one she ever talked to. She told me about springtime in her village in the valley, about the days when she was young and people called her the prettiest girl in the parish. Then her face would grow long with sadness as she told how her father had given her to Maugis the shepherd—my father—in payment of a gambling debt. When the talk turned to the babies she bore every year, the little innocents who always died before Christmas, her dismay was painful to watch. The infants were buried side by side on the far end of the village churchyard.

I might have sometimes tried to say, "Don't cry, Mother," in my useless voice. But by the time I was three years old, I'd given up speaking. After enough ridicule, after enough blows to the side of the head, even the stupidest creature stops trying. And I was never stupid. My mother knew that. She assured me of it every day when she was alive.

"The Lord may have tied your tongue so that you cannot speak," she would tell me, "but He has indeed given you a strong mind to think with. It's better to know things and not speak, Aran, than to know nothing and shout out foolishness and evil." She didn't say,

"Like your father does; like your brother does," but that's what she meant. My mother and I had learned to share our thoughts without speaking them aloud.

"In 1106, the year you were born, Aran," she often told me, "an ever-growing comet appeared each evening at sunset. It arrived on a Friday, the first week of Lent, and for the next few weeks it filled the sky with a beam of light that shone from southwest to northeast. Not till it faded on Good Friday did I give birth to you—the longest I ever carried a child. I knew it was a sign that you would be very bright, yet your brightness will be hidden, except to those who see with their hearts."

No other comets ever appeared to her. Each year, when she grew large with child, my mother's body would grow more frail. Each winter, when she buried the infant under the snow, her spirit would grow weaker.

The autumn I was eleven years old, my mother's arms were as narrow as sticks. Her legs, though, became terribly swollen from cold and from the burden she bore as her belly grew bigger. I would sit on the cold earthen floor at her feet and, with long strips of cloth, wrap her legs tightly to ease the pain. Then she would stroke my hair with her fingers, which were as thin now as broom straws.

"Aran," she would say, "you are my only happiness. After I'm gone—and that will be soon, my dear son—you must go away from this place. Otherwise they'll destroy you, as they've destroyed me." I knew she meant my father and my brother, Eustace, who was my father all over again, in looks and in brutality.

I couldn't imagine how I would ever leave the chalk cliffs. Where would I go? All I knew how to do was tend sheep. And to spin—my mother had taught me that, when no one was watching.

Then—everything happened so fast! I found myself on the road to Paris before I'd even crawled out from the great grief that crushed me after my mother's death.

It was only when she died that my father seemed to know what he'd lost. He wept real tears, and roared out an anguish that echoed off the cliffs beside our bend in the river Seine. With no one to spin the wool from that spring's shearing (he'd never learned that I could spin), he worried about the payment, due soon, to the bishop of Rouen, who owned the land we lived on.

For the first time, I saw that my father was filled with demons, and one of them was fear. With my mother gone, he'd been left with no centering to his hard life. Now he had only Eustace, my cruel brother, and me: Aran the dumb, Aran the mute, the son who shamed him, the son he never spoke to without a curse.

The son who could spin yarn as fine as any my mother had ever made, but my father didn't know that. Inside my head, I argued whether I should let him see what I could do. If I didn't, he would not be able to pay his yearly rent to the bishop of Rouen, and we would be thrown off the land.

"Go away from this place," my mother had told me. I wanted to go, but not with my father and brother. If I left, I wanted *them* to stay.

So I began to spin.

CHAPTER TWO

On the hills above the bend in the Seine, every year was the same as every other. In spring, the shearing of the sheep. Late summer, when all the fleece had been spun, the journey to Paris to sell the yarn. My brother and father traveled it on foot and were gone for ten days, a time of bliss for me. Not only was I free of their tyranny; I was freed from the job of tending the sheep.

I spent those ten days at the village church. Not to pray—I've never been much of a one for praying—but to deliver the yearly rent due for the use of our pastures.

"You go, Aran," my mother would tell me. "Stay for as long as the priest will let you. Don't worry about the sheep. I'll see to them."

I used to think she let me escape because she

wanted to be kind to me. As I grew older, I realized that her reasons were twofold: She wanted me to learn as much as I could whenever I had the chance. But perhaps even more important to her, she loved being by herself for those ten days, with no one to fix food for, no shouting to cringe from, no demands on her body from my father.

Other tenants paid their land rent with wool or lambs or firewood. We paid with yarn, because the bishop ordered us to. We learned that the bishop of Rouen had all his undergarments woven from the yarn my mother had spun, and from hers only, because it was the finest in the entire bishopric.

I was no older than six the first time Mother sent me to the priest's house, with my small arms full of yarn for the bishop's underwear.

"What's this? What's this? Is it little Aran, the mute?" Father Mattieu asked in his soft voice. "Come in, come in, child. Anastace, bring the child some bread and milk."

Anastace was the lay cleric, the young man Father Mattieu taught in those days. Many years before, Father Mattieu had been a famous preacher, with a parish in the land of Navarre. Back then, or so we heard, his voice could thunder so loud that the ceiling beams of his church would quiver and splinter. People came from everywhere to hear him preach. Then Father Mattieu became afflicted with a terrible cough. Whenever he raised his voice to preach, his thin body would be racked with such fits of coughing that sweat ran down his face and dripped from his chin like raindrops—I've heard him tell that part of it himself. As long as he kept his voice to a whisper, he never coughed at all, but what good is a preacher who can barely murmur? He came north, to our tiny village of Les Andelys, where the people needed a priest and didn't care if he was as toneless as a rock, provided he could perform the sacraments.

I think Father Mattieu liked me because I was even more silent than he was. "Come, come, little Aran," he would whisper, "sit over in the corner until you've finished your meal." Then he'd resume the lesson I'd interrupted, beginning once again to tutor Anastace, and both of them would forget that I was there.

For ten days at the end of every summer, I sat in the cool corner shadows of that church, straining to hear Father Mattieu as he spoke hardly louder than a sigh. That was how I learned to understand the Latin tongue—on those long, happy days, and on the mornings when I went to Mass with my mother, which happened only rarely, in spite of the many saints' days and holy days of obligation that filled the calendar.

From time to time, Father Mattieu or Anastace would notice me and say, "Look! Little Aran is still sitting in the corner." Then they would smile at each other in amusement, and once more bring me bread and milk, or cheese and porridge, as if I were a stray cat who'd wandered inside and stayed to be fed. Mostly, though, it was as if I were invisible. Throughout my life, I've usually been unnoticed, like a spider on the wall.

Then came the terrible year of 1118, when my mother died, and that spring I spun all the yarn myself. My father had become convinced we were cursed, because not long after we laid my mother's body into the churchyard beside her many dead infants, my father tripped in a rain-soaked ditch and broke his leg.

"You'll have to take Aran to Paris with you to sell the yarn," my father told my brother.

"Aran! What good would he do?" Eustace argued. "He's small, and besides that, he's stupid!"

"Don't defy me!" my father roared. "Do you think I can hobble on a lame leg while carrying a heavy load on my back? Aran will go, and that's the end of it!"

For the next few days Eustace scowled and grumbled, "What good is he? Dumb as a post and weak as a baby. Father should have dropped him off the cliffs long ago. Yes, you, Aran!" he'd shout as I scuttled out of his way.

My heart began to beat quicker as the time drew near for us to depart. I'd never seen any of the world other than our chalk hills and our village a few miles away, where the church stood. But I'd heard Father Mattieu talk about the huge city of Paris. Forty thousand people lived there! I couldn't even imagine what that would be like, having so many people so close together in the same place.

We started out on a clear, early autumn day, when the trees were first turning to flame like the fires of hell Father Mattieu always whispered about. Eustace made me carry most of the load, but I didn't care; unlike what he said about me, I wasn't weak at all. I balanced the bundles easily on my back.

The road from Rouen to Paris led mainly through forest, so travelers tended to join with one another en route, for protection from thieves by day and from wolves by night. I knew no harm would come to me if I stayed near Eustace. He looked so angry and vicious that not even a wolf would dare to cross his path.

At night, small groups of travelers built fires together, then gathered around them, talking, sharing food, and singing. If I hadn't been so heartsick over my mother's death—only four months earlier—I would have enjoyed those evenings. I loved the blackness of the night, when the stars rose up like flakes of oatmeal boiling in a pot, swelling and thickening until they nearly touched each other in the sky. Eustace always took all the yarn, both his bundle and mine, to make a soft bed for himself, but I never minded the bare earth beneath me.

The songs were the part I liked best. They were an amazement to me, because until then I hadn't heard anything except church hymns. The ballads travelers sang there in the forest next to the road told of beautiful ladies and valiant knights who fought brave battles. Most astonishing, the words were not in Latin, but in our own northern tongue, the *langue d'oil*, the language I would have spoken if I had spoken at all.

One night one of the travelers brought out a lute. He didn't play it very well, but at the time I knew so little about music that to me it could have been the choirs of heaven:

> "Dear lady, for your love I pray,
> To you I sing this roundelay,
> Don't scorn me, my beloved. . . ."

I felt warmed by the human sounds that drifted in the dark. After the music stopped, I heard low murmurings of men and women, with bursts of soft laughter from time to time, and the shallow, drunken snores of my brother, who'd stolen a skin of wine from an old woman we'd passed earlier in the day.

On the third afternoon, as we came closer to Paris, I could feel excitement in the very dust of the road. Large numbers of people thronged there, pulling carts full of children and turnips, pushing barrows of animal hides for the tannery, driving goats, whipping donkeys, carrying racks of dried salted fish. I drowned happily in the sea of vocal sounds—people calling to one another or arguing, animals braying, children laughing or crying, depending on whether they were large children or small. Birds squawked, clucked, and chirped in woven willow cages; fowl honked or quacked as they waddled along the edge of the road on webbed feet, driven by small boys with sticks. I think that even if I'd known how to talk, I'd have been too overwhelmed to make a sound.

"Stay right next to me," Eustace snarled. "You're so small, you could get trampled, and I still need you. You can get trampled on the way home and it won't matter." When my footsteps slowed because there was so much to see, he yanked my hair to hurry me along. I had a lot of hair to yank—thick and so black, it looked almost blue, like our mother's had. Eustace was blond and hairy like our father. Though he'd just turned nineteen, he already had a rough, shaggy beard.

We came to the river, the very same Seine that flowed past our little village of Les Andelys. If we'd had money to pay for passage, we could have floated on a barge all the way from Les Andelys to Paris, but poor people like us were used to walking everywhere we went.

A bridge called the Grand Pont spanned the Seine from its right bank to the Ile de la Cité, the island in the center where Paris stood. I had never before walked on a bridge. No matter how hard my brother, Eustace, pulled my hair to make me cross it, I balked and stood unbudging right in the middle to watch the broad waters of the Seine glide beneath me. It must feel like this to sail in a tall ship, I thought, the way the Crusaders did on their journey to the Holy Lands.

"Get moving, stupid!" Eustace shouted, right into my ear as if I were stone deaf. Reluctantly, I let him drag me the rest of the way across the Grand Pont into Paris itself.

CHAPTER THREE

$\diamond\!\!\!\!\diamond\!\!\!\!\diamond$

IF THE DUSTY HIGHWAY HAD SEEMED EXOTIC, filled with noisy peasants on their way to market, Paris was a fantasy beyond anything I could have imagined. Fishmongers and vegetable hawkers bustled through the streets, crying out their wares. Women held out baskets to butchers, who sliced off hunks of raw meat and dropped them in. Merchants guarded stalls filled with cloth, or pottery, or wax tablets for students to write on.

And the students! Black-gowned, they swarmed everywhere, drinking, brawling, and yelling in tongues I'd never heard before. Later I learned to tell the tongues apart—German, Flemish, English, Italian, Spanish, and the strange French called *langue d'oc* that was spoken in the south. But that day I felt I'd been swallowed inside a huge bell that boomed with undecipherable peals, clanging and echoing around my head, making it whirl.

Someone shouted, "Make way! Make way!" Horses clopped on cobblestones while foot soldiers, with daggers stuck in their belts, used the flat sides of their swords to push back crowds. The men approaching on horseback wore tunics the color of blood or rust or heather. But the brightest robe of all—royal purple—covered the bulging torso of a horseman wearing a crown.

"It's the king, Louis the Fat," my brother said, pushing himself in front of me. Being small, I was able to squirm around Eustace to get a good look at Louis VI, the king of France, on his way to his granite castle not more than a hundred yards from where we stood.

"Stop gawking," my brother ordered. "I want to be rid of this yarn. Stay right beside me. We'll go to the cloth-maker's house."

Snaking through the crowds was not easy. I made sure to follow close behind Eustace, who was big and rude enough to knock aside anyone who got in his way.

The cloth-maker's narrow house looked dim on the inside, dusty from tiny bits of fiber that floated up from the looms and hung in the air. Several hungry-looking men and women worked the looms. They didn't bother to glance up when we entered, but kept shuttling the yarn back and forth, back and forth, tamping it down to a tight weave. Because I was intent on watching the yarn become cloth, I paid no attention to what went on between my brother and the cloth-maker.

Suddenly, with his left hand, Eustace grabbed me by the back of my neck to drag me outside again, into the bright, noisy street. His right fist was clenched tightly around the coins the cloth-maker had given him.

With no load on my back now, I felt so weightless that I could have floated. I wanted to see more of Paris. I wanted to see everything, but Eustace had other ideas.

Still keeping hold of me by my neck, he walked me fast to an old stone building that stood in ruins, its roof collapsed, the floor filled with rubble. "Get in here and stay put," he told me. "Don't move a foot out of here. I'll be back after a while, and if you're not here, you'll be sorry."

I picked my steps carefully through the broken boards and fallen tiles, looking for a place to sit. When I turned around, Eustace was gone. Leaning against what remained of a wall, I pulled my knees against my chest, circled them with my arms, and stared up. Straight up, since the building had no roof.

By then evening had come. The sky above Paris was clear blue tinged with pink—that soft, just-before-sunset sky that never looks as lovely anywhere else. I was hungry. Maybe Eustace had gone to buy food for the two of us. But probably not.

A face, pale except for the ruddy, wrinkled

cheeks, peered over the broken wall to stare at me. "Dear boy, what are you doing in there?" the man asked, bending closer as though he couldn't quite see. "It's not safe. Come out of there at once."

I scrambled to my feet.

He was quite old, and he wore the black robe of a priest. Thick white hair ringed his head, except for the top, which had been shaved clean. All men connected to the Church—whether they were priests, deacons, canons, or even if they were teachers, since all the schools belonged to the Church—had to shave a clean and perfectly round circle on the tops of their heads. The tonsure showed their obedience to God.

"You must be from the countryside," the priest said, and I nodded.

"That's why you don't know it's forbidden to enter this place. This is the Basilica of Saint-Etienne le Vieux. Or it *was*. It was built six hundred years ago and now it's nothing but ruins, so it's no longer used. And it's dangerous in there." The priest chattered on, not seeming to mind that I didn't answer. Holding out his hand to me, he said, "If you need a place to stay for the night, you can go inside the cathedral. It's right over there."

I didn't move.

"Come, boy," he said. "You're tempting the wrath of God. It could fall down on your head in the form of a roof tile." He squinted up. "Though there are few enough tiles hanging on up there these days."

The threat of a roof dropping on me wasn't nearly as frightening as the thought of what Eustace would do to me if he came back and I wasn't there. But I could see that the priest was trying to be kind. I decided to go with him. As soon as he left me, I'd return to this ruined Basilica of Saint-Etienne the Old and wait for Eustace.

"You see," the priest said as he led me forward, "our Carolingian Cathedral is much newer—it was built only two and a half centuries ago. A mere babe among buildings." He laughed at his own joke. "That's the one I'm taking you to—the Cathedral of Notre Dame. It's ugly and not much of a monument to Our Lady, the Mother of Christ, is it? But the whole thing is made of wood, so it may one day burn down around our ears. And that could be a good thing," he added, chuckling. "The bishop of Paris says he wants to tear down this cathedral and build a much more magnificent one right here on this same spot. An enormous, brand-new Cathedral of Notre Dame, all made of stone. But he can't afford it."

Patting me on the head, he said, "Still, it might happen in your lifetime, little boy. Who knows what wonderful things men can accomplish when God wills it."

In the priest's dim eyesight, I must have seemed only seven or eight since I was still so small, even though I was now twelve years old. No wonder he was being kind to me—he thought I was a lost waif. I smiled up at him.

He opened the heavy, carved door for me. "Stay in here, now," he said. "When I see a mother looking for her little boy, I'll tell her where you are." With a gentle wave, he left me there.

To me, the cathedral was not ugly at all. As I stood just inside the door, letting my eyes adjust to the dimness, I thought it looked pretty, and quite large compared to our village church in Les Andelys. Slowly, I walked forward toward the front altar, taking big steps and counting as I went. Sixty steps: sixty yards in length from back to front.

Dozens of wax candles burned on tall holders, illuminating the stone altarpiece. The air was so still, the flames neither wavered nor flickered. Dazzled by their light, I didn't at first notice the young woman who knelt in prayer. Then she stood, and I wondered how I ever could have missed noticing her. Or how anyone could have.

Her hair hung long and dark from beneath a short cloth headdress. The loose-hanging hair was a sign that she was unmarried, although she appeared old enough for marriage. About seventeen or eighteen, I thought.

Tall, perfectly formed, she held herself as straight as a queen. But no queen had ever looked more beautiful than this girl did. Her long fingers laced together in prayer just beneath her full breasts, and her sleeves fell back to show the smooth roundness of her arms.

Even if I'd been given to speech, I'd have been

struck dumb anyway by this exquisite girl. As it was, I stood rooted to the floor, unable to stop staring at her. Then I realized there was one additional person in the cathedral. A man, standing behind me, who turned toward me and smiled.

That smile! It was the first time anyone had ever looked at me as though I were someone who mattered. As if he were saying to me, without words, "Because you and I are men, we appreciate feminine beauty when we see it."

From that moment, I couldn't take my eyes from the man! He was just as perfect, in a masculine way, as the woman was beautiful. His hair shone golden in the candles' gleam. Slight in build, not very tall, he wore the black gown of a scholar, but the gown looked richly made, not at all like the shabby gowns of the students on the streets.

When he stepped forward as though to get a better look at the girl, his movements were spare and controlled with no wasted motion, showing tight command over bone and muscle. Though not large, he seemed powerful.

She turned then. Without a glance at either of us and with her hands still folded, she walked the length of the stone floor to the cathedral doors. The man waited until the door closed behind her, then he followed. Just before he stepped out into the Parisian evening, he looked back over his shoulder and once more smiled at me.

Not a word had been spoken by any of us, but when they were gone and I was all alone, I felt desolate because I thought I would never see them again.

There was no way for me to know then how enmeshed I would become in the web that linked Abelard and Eloise.

CHAPTER FOUR

I HAD NO PLACE TO GO except back to the ruins of
Saint-Etienne. Hunger gnawed at me, but since
hunger had stalked the shadows of our hut every
single winter, I'd learned to tolerate it. I found a spot
clear of rubble and lay on my back to watch the stars
come out.

Hours later, I heard Eustace cursing as he stumbled through the broken stones. Drunk as he was, I
don't know how he'd found his way back to the basilica. He fell to the ground and slept instantly.

In the darkness, I crept toward him. His rucksack lay beside him; I felt inside it to discover
whether he'd brought any food. The sack was empty.
No food, and not a single coin. What had happened
to the money we'd been paid for the yarn?

Worried, I slipped my hand inside his belt,

searching for any piece of twisted cloth that might have contained the money. Nothing. And nothing inside his tunic.

I rolled him over to see if he'd slid the coins underneath him. He was so deeply sunken into his wine-sodden stupor that I could have set him on his head and he wouldn't have wakened. Next I took off his shoes, but no coins rattled inside them. Perhaps he'd hidden the money under a stone somewhere. If that's what he'd done, I hoped he'd remember which stone it was when he came back to life in the morning.

Hours later, I was awakened by the tolling of the cathedral bell of Notre Dame. Eustace still snored, dead to the world. In the early light I got my first good view of him; he looked as though someone had rolled him down a rock quarry—bruised, crusted with blood from small cuts, his face filthy and his clothes torn. From past experience I knew he'd wake up in a rage and start to beat me, since I was his closest target. I might have stayed and resigned myself to the beating, but just then I looked over the wall and saw the girl, the beautiful one from the cathedral.

Cautiously, I shook my brother's shoulder, trying to guess how close he was to waking up. His eyelids didn't even flutter, which meant he'd probably sleep for another hour or two. Leaving him to his dreams, I climbed over the crumbled wall and followed the girl, who was on her way to Mass, alone, without any servant or chaperone to watch over her. I wondered if she planned to meet the man who'd admired her the evening before.

As soon as I slipped through the heavy door, I saw him, too, dressed again in the same rich black robe. Later I would learn to distinguish the gown of a teacher from the students' plainer gowns, even though all of them wore black. This man was a teacher, although he didn't appear scholarly. He stood with his fists on his hips and his legs spread apart like a young warrior. Chin thrust forward, head tilted back, he looked not exactly arrogant, but supremely confident.

Behind him, a group of students jostled for position, trying to get close to him, like sparrows fighting over crumbs. As the lovely, tall girl walked past to stand near the altar, the man's eyes followed every step she took. Some of the students watched the girl but most of them glanced back and forth from the girl to the man, eyes on her, then on him—it was no wonder! The two of them were like a god and goddess who'd descended from above the clouds. Compared to them, every other person in the cathedral blurred into shadowy insignificance.

They exchanged no words at all. She didn't as much as turn her head in his direction. But he never stopped looking at her.

After the Mass ended, the man left the cathedral with his hordes of students still fluttering around him. For the first time, I heard him speak.

"The sun is warm," he said. "I will lecture outside today."

His deep, rich voice caused a bustle of activity among his students. Some of them ran around the corner—I didn't know why. Soon they returned carrying a chair and shouting, "Get out of the way. Here's Master Abelard's chair!" Knocking one another aside, they set a tall carved armchair against the sunniest wall of the cathedral. "Master Peter," they called out. "Master Abelard, will you begin?" That was how I learned his name: Peter Abelard.

He sat on the chair, letting his gown fall open, crossing his legs to show that he was wearing bright green leggings. From the way the students pointed and laughed, I could guess that a teaching master was not supposed to wear bright colors, and that they loved him all the better for his defiance. More and more students poured out of the side streets to sit at his feet. They kept coming, their black gowns flapping, until at least two hundred crowded together, seating themselves shoulder to shoulder on the packed earth. A few had brought straw to sit on. Some held wax tablets and styluses to write with. Others, the wealthier ones, carried pieces of parchment rolled into scrolls.

Most were young, some not a lot older than I was. More than a few looked underfed; many wore torn, tattered gowns, but all of them sat there in the warmth of that autumn morning in happy, noisy anticipation, full of high spirits, waiting for Master Peter Abelard to speak. They looked up at him as if he were the sun.

When Master Abelard began to lecture in Latin, I wiggled forward, keeping on the edge of the crowd but working my way toward the front. I understood his words, but not their meaning—what he was teaching went far beyond my small smattering of learning.

Suddenly, I realized I'd begun to comprehend a little of what he said. One of the students had challenged Master Abelard on some point of argument or other. When Abelard answered, I noticed a slight edge to his resonant voice—not the razor sharpness of a sword, but more like the blade of a small fruit-paring knife. No one else may have noticed it, but I did, because although I never spoke, I listened intently, and I caught things other people missed.

Smoothly, almost gently, gazing through half-lowered eyelids at the young man who'd challenged him, Master Abelard began to demolish him, slice by slice, shredding the helpless student with his tongue until the boy's cheeks flamed blood red.

"Dialectic, Joachim," Abelard drawled, letting his arms hang loosely over the sides of the chair as though to show that publicly humiliating a student didn't take much effort, and didn't even require the master to sit up straight. "Dialectic means logic, Joachim, which your question shows a pathetic lack of. Were you ever taught logic? Or did you live in a cave with animals? Even the youngest child senses logic, Joachim. God instills it in us at birth. But maybe God missed you somehow."

"I—I—," the student stammered.

In a singsong voice Abelard began to chant:

> *"Si sol est, et lux est; at sol est: igitur lux.*
> *Si non sol, non lux est; at lux est: igitur sol.*
> *Non est sol et non-lux; at sol est: igitur lux."*

How many times had I heard Father Mattieu repeat that same verse in his soft voice as he tried to teach logic to Anastace! Without thinking, I smiled and moved my head from side to side to match the rhythm of the lines:

> "If there is sun, there is light; since now
> there is sun: therefore there is light.
> If there is no sun, there is no light; since
> there is light now: there must be sun.
> No sun is no light; now there is sun: so
> there must be light."

And on and on. Those simple, lilting lines were sung to schoolboys to help them memorize; Abelard was using them now to mock this unfortunate scholar who'd dared to challenge him. Suddenly Abelard leaped from his chair and rushed straight toward me, pointing at me as he came.

"Even this little street vagabond understands logic," he cried. "Stand up, urchin, and recite the poem to these empty-headed scholars. I can tell that you know it."

My eyes opened wide in astonishment as my mouth dropped open in dismay. Thrusting his hands beneath my arms, Abelard lifted me high, preparing to turn me around like a puppet to perform in front of the crowd. But as he lifted me, he noticed the inside of my wide-open mouth, and saw how rigidly my tongue was stuck to the flesh beneath it.

Immediately the mockery drained from Abelard's face. Still holding me up, he said, "No, I will not make this peasant child recite dialectic to you ignoramuses. He's too bright to waste his gifts on the lot of you. But he knows the verse. I saw it in his eyes just a moment ago. No doubt God put it there."

He set me down, then strode back to his chair. As he arranged himself so that his bright green leggings showed, he once again gave me that brief conspirator's smile, the same way he'd looked at me in the cathedral the night before. In that instant he became my hero. I knew I would walk through fire for him, would lay down my life for him.

How quickly my emotions soared—and then crashed! When Abelard had lifted me up, I'd been thunderstruck, then frightened, then ready to idolize him. Now, before I could even catch my breath, I was plunged into the worst humiliation of my life.

My brother, Eustace, lurched into view—still half drunk, filthy, and foul-smelling. "There you are, you worthless piece of sheep droppings!" he yelled at me. "I told you not to move from that place!" He yanked me up by the hair, but that pain was nothing compared to my shame that Master Abelard should see such a spectacle.

"The boy's caused no harm here," Abelard told Eustace. "He's listening to my lecture."

"What! *Him!* He's stupid. A dummy. A mute. Can't talk at all." Stumbling in his drunkenness, Eustace grimaced and stuck out his tongue. "Blaaa, blaaa, blaaa—he used to talk like that when he was a baby. Blaaa, blaaa—that was all he could say, but Papa beat him so bad, his brains got broken. If he ever had any."

The students had begun to roar with laughter at Eustace. "Blaaa, blaaa, blaaa," they mimicked him. The ones in back jumped up to see over the heads of the others, and all of them angled for a better look at this unwashed, ludicrous, bearded, half-drunk lout who'd stumbled into their lecture.

Eustace grabbed for me; I scrambled away. He caught my foot and flung me on my back; the students hooted even louder. Even Master Abelard had to smile when I struggled to escape as Eustace hauled me off bodily, dragging me by the neck of my tunic so that my head was covered, my bare belly showed, and my heels gouged grooves in the dust. I was glad my face was hidden then, because all I wanted was to die of shame.

He hoisted me and carried me under his arm the way he'd carry a lamb toward slaughter. "Wha'd you want to be around *them* for?" he asked, cursing. "They're nothing but a bunch of thieves! Got me drunk last night and stole all my money. Papa will kill me if I come home without money, even if I tell him it's your fault." Breaking into a trot, he panted as he said, "But if I come home without *you*—!" His laugh was ugly. "He won't care! And I found a place to sell you, so I'll have some money to show Papa."

I didn't believe that and, anyway, I didn't care what he did with me. He could drop me into the river and it wouldn't matter. He began to run, jostling me up and down like a sack of turnips. When he finally set me on the ground—keeping tight hold of me so I couldn't bolt—we were in front of a wide house on a strangely quiet street.

Eustace still looked terrible, but his head seemed to have cleared. Clamping me with one hand, he banged on the door. When it opened, I stared into the face of an old woman no taller than I was.

"Where's Master Galien?" Eustace demanded.

"I'll fetch him," she answered in a voice as deep as a man's. It sounded too big to come out of that small, twisted body. She eyed us suspiciously. "Wait outside."

After a long stretch of time when Eustace's fingers

dug into my shoulders hard enough to leave bruises, the door opened again. A small man, totally bald, with piercing black eyes, peered out at us. He wore a food-stained tunic of rich red cloth. "Well?" he asked.

"I'm selling my brother," Eustace stated.

"Why should that interest me?"

"I heard that you buy and sell freaks, and my brother's a freak."

The man looked mildly interested. "In what way?"

When Eustace pried open my mouth, I didn't resist, not even after he shoved a filthy finger inside. "See? His tongue can't move. He can't talk."

"Tongue-tied? That's nothing," the man said, starting to close the door.

Eustace, glowering, managed to look murderous. He shoved hard against the door, blocking it open. I could see the man recoil in alarm.

"I need money!" Eustace demanded. "Take him and give me money." He pushed me forward with such force, I smacked against the man, who grabbed me to keep both of us from falling.

"Four silver sous!" the man cried. "And he isn't worth two, so don't ask for more. And you won't even get the four if you don't leave this place right now!" He threw the money into the street, then slammed the door in my brother's face.

I half expected Eustace to start bellowing or pounding again, but all stayed silent. Holding me at arm's length, the man examined me with distaste. "How old are you?" he asked.

I shook my head.

"If you are too stupid to learn, I'll sell you right away to the coal miners. They'll strap you to a cart and make you haul coal until you die, which should take about three months. If you want to live, show me right now that you understand what I say."

With Eustace gone, the prospect of living awhile longer didn't seem as bleak. I nodded.

"All right," the man said, and called out, "Flore! Come here."

When the stunted, twisted old woman appeared, he told her, "Take this child and clean him. Then lock him in a room until I decide what to do with him. Are you hungry?" he suddenly asked me.

I nodded again.

"Feed him something," he told Flore. "He's so small, he's probably been poorly fed most of his life. Feed him well. Hmmmm . . ." He tapped his lip with two fingers. "An idea is coming to me. Tongue-tied is worth nothing, but . . . perhaps . . ." He smiled. "We could use another spider."

His words made no sense.

CHAPTER FIVE

WITH EVERYTHING THAT HAD HAPPENED, it was surprising I could care about food. When Flore brought me a big bowl of stew and a small loaf of bread, I devoured them like someone who was famished. They tasted wonderful. The stew was full of meat and fish and onions and other vegetables I didn't recognize, all flavored by a thick brown broth. I ate every spoonful, then cleaned the bowl with bits of bread that I stuffed into my mouth.

In her deep voice, Flore told me that the man who bought me was called Galien of Laon. "He bought me, too," she said, "when I was young like you. Twenty years ago."

That would mean Flore was now not much more than thirty, yet she seemed ancient. Her skin was creased and filled with moles and hairy warts. Her teeth were yellow and fanglike, and her head sat so low in her shoulders it looked like an egg in a nest.

"I had a sister who was tongue-tied like you," she told me. "My papa left her out in the snow to die. I don't know why they kept me. Maybe because I had a good nose to smell out truffles in the forest. I could root them up like a pig."

Bewildered, I just stared at her.

"No, a boy like you wouldn't understand about truffles," she went on. "They're delicacies, wonderful mushrooms that grow beneath the soil. You can't see them—you have to sense them. Like this." She sniffed to demonstrate, wrinkling her nose. "By the time I lost the power to smell them out, I'd become a good cook, and my father sold me to Galien. It didn't matter that I was ugly. The uglier a person is, the better Galien likes them." She chuckled in her deep, rough voice, although I didn't know why what she'd said should seem funny.

"Here's a blanket to keep you warm," she told me. "In the morning I'll bring you extra food."

These strange people were treating me more kindly than my father or brother ever had. As she left, I heard her slide a heavy bolt across the outside of the door. I was locked in.

The room had no windows, so I couldn't tell how many hours had passed. I tried to hear the cathedral bells, but all sound was muffled. Sometimes I thought I heard odd, high-pitched laughter, though I couldn't be sure. Wrapping the blanket around me, I sat and thought about Abelard.

The way he spoke! That rich, full tone, the mouth that shaped words as God must have meant them to be uttered. If only I could speak that way! If only I could speak at all. I vowed then that I would never again show that I understood Latin, because it had brought me such humiliation that day. People knew I was mute; let them believe I was stupid, too.

Except—Master Galien said that if I were too stupid, he'd sell me to the coal miners. If I were clever, he had something else in store for me. What could it be? Galien bought and sold freaks, Eustace said. I was small and silent, but I didn't look at all strange. The woman Flore was ugly, yet Galien hadn't sold her. I couldn't find any pattern to it. There was nothing for me to do but wait.

I must have been tired; I slept until I heard the bolt slide back. The door creaked open, and Master Galien himself came into the room.

Saying nothing, he tossed a wooden ball at me, and I instinctively reached out to catch it. Then he threw another ball, and a third, and a fourth, which I also caught. "Toss them back," he ordered me, and I did. As he left the room, I heard him mutter, "Quick hands."

It grew more and more puzzling. The next time Master Galien came, he brought along another man, large, burly, and soot-stained.

"This is Tancred," he told me. "He's come to

measure you for new clothes." The man named Tancred chuckled at that, in the same way Flore had chuckled earlier.

I couldn't imagine why a tailor would be so large and heavily muscled and dirty. After he told me to stand up, he began to measure me with a cord. First he wrapped it around my chest and tied a knot to mark the length. Then he repeated it, running the cord around my hips, knotting it and, after that, stretching it from my shoulder to my groin.

Grunting when it was over, he balled up the cord in his big fist and left the room, followed by Master Galien, who bolted the door again.

Not much later Flore arrived with a bowl and more bread. "Pottage," she said, pointing into the bowl, "with leeks, cabbage, onions, garlic, and lots of good beef marrow to make you grow. Master Galien wants you to grow fast. Eat all of it."

Before she closed the door behind her, I heard it again—the high-pitched giggles. It sounded as though a dozen or more children were in the house, playing and laughing. But I'd been told to eat, so I did, although before I reached the bottom of the bowl I felt too full. I wasn't used to so much food.

Again, the hours dragged. Flore came once more to bring me a slop bucket, which I badly needed by then, and she left it in the room with me. I wondered how I was supposed to empty it, or who else might be obliged to empty it, since I was locked up.

It was impossible to tell how much time had passed when the door opened once more. This time Flore came in carrying a brazier filled with burning coals. I thought she must be going to cook something right in my room, but then Tancred followed with what looked like a small suit of armor—just the top part.

"First, take off your tunic," Tancred told me, "then try this on for size."

I didn't move, except to stare from the burning coals to the curved metal corselet in Tancred's hands, wondering if the two of them went together in some way.

"Take off your—"

With surprising strength, Flore grabbed me and pulled my tunic over my head. It ripped as it came off. "We'll get you a new one," she said. "You'll have lots of new clothes." Then, clutching my thighs in a viselike grip so I couldn't move, she said soothingly, "Don't struggle. It will be over soon, and I'll bring you fresh pastry with apples and honey."

I struggled anyway, but it was useless. Tancred lifted my arms straight up and slid the metal sheath over me; it reached from my shoulders to my hips, encasing me like a turtle's shell. Then, with tongs, he poked at some metal links lying on top of the coals on the brazier.

My eyes grew wide with fright. Was I going to be branded? Marked like a thief?

Tancred fitted one of the red-hot, bendable links through holes in the top edges of the sheath. I tried to scream from the searing heat on my shoulder but instead I fainted from the pain. As I lost consciousness I heard Flore say, "He's gone; now it will be easier to do."

What happened next I could only imagine. I awakened with my eyelashes glued shut from the salt of my tears, unable to think because of unbearable torment. Flore sat next to me, dripping cool water onto my severely burned shoulders and groin. "If you don't get blood poisoning and die," she said, "the burns will heal in a few weeks. I have special herbs to hasten the healing."

I was encased in metal from shoulders to hips, with chain links fused across my shoulders and between my legs so that I could not free myself from this shell. Why? Why would they do this to me, I wondered, before I turned my head to the wall and lost consciousness again.

The days—or maybe a week—passed in feverishness and nightmares. Flore seemed to be with me most of the time, smearing potions on my burns or holding herbs against them, and always urging me to eat. The most I could swallow was a thin broth.

One day—I don't know how long afterward— she propped me up against the wall and said, "I want you to move your arms. Raise them."

When I did, she told me, "I've done a good job on you. You'll be scarred, but you haven't lost any motion. Do you know why that matters? Because you're going to be a juggler."

I looked at her vacantly, too wretched to be surprised by anything.

"And not just a street juggler," she went on. "Galien will train you himself, then sell you to a nobleman. Maybe even to the king." Turning away from me she shouted, "Come in now, Rabel, and show this boy what he's going to become."

The door must have no longer been kept bolted, probably because I was too weak to escape, even if I'd wanted to. A strange creature came toward me, a boy with hair so blond it was almost white, and pink-rimmed eyes with no color at all in the irises. He had a thin face, and arms and legs far too long for his short torso. Giggling, he bowed toward me and said, "I'm Rabel, the human spider." He lifted his tunic to show that he was encased in the same kind of metal shroud that I was.

"Look at him," Flore told me. "See the shape of him—all arms and legs. Like a spider. Perform for us, Rabel," she said.

The boy lifted a lute and strummed it. In a high, reedy voice he began to sing,

> "Give me a keepsake, my sweeting,
> A kerchief your lips may have brushed,
> And if war shall force us apart,
> Till my heart is no longer beating,
> And all of my bones have been crushed,
> Your token will lie on my heart.

On my heart, all broken and bleeding.
On my poor, dying heart."

Flore shrugged. "Perhaps not the best singing voice ever heard," she said, "and the verse is mediocre—he wrote it himself. But none of that matters. Rabel is a real oddity. A rich nobleman will pay handsomely for him."

"Handsomely! That means for a great deal of money," Rabel giggled, balancing on his toes.

To me, Flore said, "And one day you will be just like Rabel, except that you will juggle balls in the air, rather than sing."

Be like that misshapen boy? My eyes filled with horror.

"Master Galien has trained Rabel for four years now," she went on. "It was four years ago Rabel was encased in a carapace like the one you're wearing, boy—I wish I knew your name; we'll have to make up a name for you. All that time Rabel has been fed the finest of food, as much as he can swallow. Since his chest and trunk and hips are squeezed tightly, they have no room to grow, so the growth goes into his arms and legs. You see?" She pointed at the grotesquely distorted singer, then told me, "One day you will look like this, too, little one. You'll be a long-armed, long-legged spider boy with hardly any body. Just like Rabel." She smiled as though giving me the good news that I would some day be crowned king.

"And Galien will sell you for a fine price."

Moaning, I thrashed on the floor as the tears ran down my cheeks.

"Why weep?" Flore asked me. "The world is a cruel place. Would you rather starve on the streets? When Master Galien finishes with you, you'll live in a grand castle. You'll be petted and fussed over by court ladies, and you'll never go hungry." She patted my cheek. "Not only that, you'll always have a warm fire to sleep beside, even in the coldest winter storms."

Hopping up and down, Rabel added, "And all you'll have to do is entertain the noble guests, like I will. Only you won't be able to sing, like I can. A juggler isn't worth nearly as much as a singer. Singing's better." He began to strum his lute again. "Sing, sing, the spider sings! I want to sing! To sing! The spider loves to sing!" As he danced happily around the room, I saw a hint of madness in his eyes.

"No more singing now, Rabel," Flore told him, waving him away. "Bring in some of the others."

I thought I must still be inside one of my nightmares. Small creatures crowded into the room: three dwarfs laughing and chattering, patting each other and pinching one another on the cheeks and buttocks; a twisted girl with missing arms whose fingers grew out of her shoulders; a hunchback with protruding teeth that curved over his tiny chin; a small child—I couldn't tell whether it was a boy or girl—whose face and arms were covered with hair like an animal's. There was a child with only one eye, in the middle of his face—and many more, but I couldn't stand to look. I squeezed my eyelids shut.

"They're worth a fortune. The odder, the better," Flore added. "Their parents are so happy to get rid of them, they beg Galien to take them, but he won't have just any ugly child. He picks only the most grotesque." She picked up one who had tripped and fallen, and set it on her knee. "And these children themselves—they're delighted to be here. We treat them with the greatest kindness while Galien trains them in courtly manners."

The children were climbing all over her now, pulling her hair out from under her cap, planting wet kisses on her hands. "Yes, yes, my little uglies," she cooed as a smile creased her deep-sunken cheeks. To me, she said, "It's a prosperous business. The rich are always desperate to be amused, so they love our little monstrosities. Over the years, some of our freaks have become famous court jesters."

Finally she pushed the children away. "All right, go away now, the lot of you." Turning back to me, she rubbed at my tears with her rough hand. "So you see, little spider, the more you eat, the faster your arms and legs will grow, and the quicker you'll find a place in some rich man's castle. You profit, and we profit."

As Flore left me, I began to shake, and I couldn't stop. Even today, when I remember those—creatures—I shake inside.

CHAPTER SIX

I REFUSED TO EAT.

Flore was beside herself. She spent hours cooking up concoctions to tempt me—fresh trout with saffron, kidney pies, quail stuffed with ground chestnuts—but I wouldn't take a single bite. Not even a sip of broth. I'd decided I would rather starve to death than turn into a gargoyle like Rabel.

My tears dried up, and now Flore was the one who wept.

"Please, little spider," she begged. "Just smell how good this is. Mmmmm, take a sniff. I made it just for you."

I turned my head away, feeling sorry not only for myself, but for Flore, too. I could see she'd become fond of me and it pained her to watch me waste away and starve myself hollow-cheeked and pale. And I think she was a little afraid that if Master Galien found out I wasn't eating, he'd grow angry and maybe beat her. Poor Flore, who had so little—hardly any pleasure in her life, no one to love her, and no family except the ugly misfit children who clustered around her. When she wept over me, my heart softened. But not enough to make me give up my stubborn refusal of food.

One day as she sat beside my pallet on the floor—trying to coax me with honey cakes, telling me about the riches in the king's palace and how lovely it would be when I was a court juggler, getting spoiled and petted by all those noble ladies—we heard a terrible commotion outside.

"This is my house," Master Galien was shouting from the hall. "Get out!"

"Where is he? Where are you hiding him?" a man's voice demanded, making my heart jolt in my chest. I'd recognize that voice at the gates of heaven or hell: Abelard!

He burst into the room, crying, "Aha! There he is," while Master Galien followed right behind him, shouting, "Get out! Get out!"

"What have you done to him?" Abelard cried. "He's nearly dead."

"He's fine!" Master Galien snapped angrily, but then he got his first good look at me in a week. The whites of his beady black eyes widened in alarm.

When Abelard bent to reach for me, Flore leaped

at him and scratched him, as ferocious as a mother cat defending her favorite kitten. "Leave him alone!" she screamed. Abelard sidestepped the attack and at the same time gave Flore a shove that knocked her to the floor. Then, as he scooped me into his arms, Abelard himself looked so fierce that Galien stepped backward to cower near the wall.

"If you want him so much—take him," Galien growled. "Only first pay me back what I paid for him. Ten sous, plus another twenty we spent on food for him." If there'd been less uproar right then, I might have smiled at that. Galien had certainly inflated his accounts.

"I won't give you as much as a copper penny, you festering pimple on a whore's backside," Abelard raged. "And if you cause me one flake of trouble, you'll find your house burned down around your ears tonight. I have students who will do anything I ask them to." He glared at Galien, who backed away even farther.

Still on her hands and knees, Flore whimpered, "Don't take him! Please don't take my little spider. He's the only pretty child I've ever had." Her tears dropped to the stone floor in great round splotches.

Abelard's lip curled with scorn, but he said nothing to her, and I was glad. Flore had tried so hard to be kind to me—yet there was no time then even to think about that. Still holding me in his arms, Abelard kicked open the door and strode through the house onto the street.

47

The bright sun blinded me. I squinted, then squeezed my eyes tightly shut, but it hardly helped — behind my eyelids, rings of light sparkled in dazzling colors as they radiated outward like waves in a pond. Abelard pulled his cloak over my face to shield it from the light. "The first thing we must do," he told me, "is find a blacksmith to strike off that iron sheath they've molded around you. I've heard about this trick of turning children into human spiders, but I've never seen it done before."

"Master Abelard!" Although my eyes were covered by his cloak, I heard the voices. No matter where Abelard went, he was recognized and followed, by his students and by any nearby street urchins who hoped to be brushed by the tiniest shadow of his fame.

"Let me carry him," one of the students said. I was shifted into someone else's arms as a young voice asked, "So you found him, then? This is the boy you wanted?"

"It's the right one, Marcel," Abelard answered. "You and the others did good work in locating him."

I pulled a corner of the hood away from my eyes so I could get a glimpse of who was carrying me. The student named Marcel was very young, probably not more than four or five years older than I was. He grinned with pleasure over Abelard's praise. "It wasn't just me," he said. "When we heard what you wanted, we spread the word to a few of the other fellows, and they asked others and so on until we tracked it down. This boy's brother, the one who sold him, had bragged about it in the tavern a few weeks ago. He came into the tavern with four silver sous, but he left with only one or two, they said, so I guess he didn't stay in Paris much longer." Marcel frowned down at me and asked, "But why did you want this particular boy, Master Abelard? He's no different from a hundred others on the streets."

I raised my head a little, because I'd begun to wonder the same thing myself.

Lowering his voice so that only Marcel could hear him, and not the others who still lagged behind, Abelard murmured, "The truth is, Marcel, at this time I need a servant who doesn't talk."

Surely he couldn't mean me! I, Aran, become a servant to someone like Abelard? How could I ever serve a master like that? I was too ignorant. I didn't know anything other than how to tend sheep.

"A servant who *cannot* talk, even if he should have certain tales to tell," Abelard added.

Marcel laughed harder this time, and began to sing some snatches of a love song. The other students joined in. Soon the whole band of youths that followed Abelard was singing in a loud, rowdy chorus, something about a woman whose skin was as soft as roses and whose breast was whiter than lilies. Abelard just smiled and commented, "That's the song I wrote only last week. How did all of you learn it so fast?"

We'd reached a street where a chapel was being built; I could hear the ring of heavy hammers striking stone. "Maybe we won't need to find a smith," Abelard said. "A man with a chisel could do it as well." He peered down at me and asked, "Do you think you can stand up?"

I nodded. But when Marcel set me on my feet, my legs buckled. "Here, let's lay him on this block of stone," Marcel said. "He's as weak as a baby."

"Foreman!" Abelard called. "You over there with the hammer. I have a job for you."

As I lay on my back staring at the sky, a sweaty workman, bare from the waist up, leaned over me. Abelard spoke softly into the man's ear; I was too dizzy to understand what they said, and anyway, they spoke in the *langue d'oc* from the south of France. Quickly, the man fitted the tip of a chisel into one of the links that fastened my iron shell across my shoulders. Then he raised his hammer.

Lying flat on the huge block of stone, looking up at that big fist coming down at me, I felt like Isaac being offered as a sacrifice by Abraham. Would the hammer dash out my brains? It hit, then, and an unbearable burst of pain made me faint. Just as I lost consciousness I heard a voice say, "He's gone. Now the rest will be easier."

I'd heard those same words before. Was it Flore's husky voice saying them again — Flore, who sounded like a man? Had it all been a dream that Abelard was taking me away to be his servant? Or was I living it all over again, being welded into the iron sheath while the red-hot, malleable chain links got forged shut across my shoulders and between my legs? How many times did I have to relive it before I could die and escape? More likely, I'd already died, and this was hell.

Slowly, I became conscious, fighting through layers of fog and pain. When my eyes at last opened, I looked up to see—not the ugly face of Flore, but the exquisite face of the girl from the cathedral. Either it was she, or I had really died, but instead of hell, I'd gone to heaven where the angels looked like her.

"Poor little fellow," she murmured as she touched my bleeding shoulders, sending shivers of agony through them. "His burn scabs got torn open from the hammer blows. Abelard, why did they put him into a metal carapace like that?"

"To turn him into a human spider, a grotesquerie they could sell to the court. For the nobles' amusement." Abelard stood on the other side of me, looking not at me but at her. "It isn't done too often, but it's not unheard of, either, Eloise. You should have seen the other monstrosities in that place."

"I wish we could rescue them all," she said.

"We'll start with this one." Then it was Abelard's fingers on me, tracing my ribs. His touch on the bare skin of my chest made me realize, for the first time, that the iron cage was gone. "He seems close to starvation—his bones push out like the edges of knives. Feed him something warm and soft, Eloise. I have to leave now for my afternoon lecture. When I return, you and I will study some lines I've copied from Plato."

She caught his hand as he turned away. "He doesn't talk, but can he understand what we say? And does he have a name?"

"Ask him."

"Tell me who you are," she murmured, leaning over me so close that her dark hair brushed my naked chest. I shook my head.

"I'll call him Spider," Abelard decided, "because that was what he nearly became."

Frowning, Eloise answered, "That's not a name. He needs a Christian name."

"Oh, he does, does he?" Abelard smiled as he told her, "When I was a boy I had a dog named 'Dog' and a cat we called 'Cat,' so I see no harm in calling this child 'Spider.' He's got such scrawny arms and legs, he looks like a spider, anyway. And like a spider, he's silent and doesn't want to tell us who he is. Unless," he added, narrowing his eyes at me, "he's able to write his name for us. Can you write, little Spider?"

I shook my head.

"The perfect servant," Abelard said softly. "Can't speak, can't write, so any secrets he learns will stay inside him, locked as tight as in a tomb. But he's bright, I can tell. Look into his eyes, Eloise. There's intelligence there."

"That's why he should have a proper name," she declared.

"He was probably christened with a proper saint's name, but if he won't tell us what it is, we can't find out, can we? I have to go now. Do your best with him. He's an odd one—he interests me. I'd like him to live."

She rose and told Abelard, "I'll walk to the door with you. Then I'll bring him something to eat. Will you eat for me, little Spider?" she asked.

I nodded, and felt my lips twist into a smile, the first I'd worn in a long time. For her, I would eat anything she brought me. For him, who had saved me, I would do my best to stay alive.

When both of them had gone, I looked around me. I was lying on a bed in what appeared to be the top floor of someone's house. Although the room was spacious, it held only the bed I lay on, a table with several candles, two chairs, and in the corner, a chest—for clothes, I supposed.

And books. They were everywhere. Stacked on the floor, flung open on the tabletop, propped on the windowsills, spilling over the seats of the chairs and the top of the clothes chest.

The room must occupy the whole top floor, I saw, because the head of the bed leaned against one wall and each of the other three walls had its own window. Two of the windows were shuttered closed, but the third, the one opposite me, stood open to let in the autumn-chilled air. Through that window I could see no other housetops. Only sky. So the house I was in evidently stood taller than its neighbors.

"Spider?" Eloise had returned, carrying a bowl of milk with bits of bread soaking in it. She wrinkled her nose as she said, "I don't like calling you that, but if it's what he wants. . . ." She propped me up against her shoulder, then held a spoonful of milk to my lips. "This will make you strong again."

I ate as slowly as possible, both because my stomach was unused to food after all that time, and because I wanted to prolong her nearness. Like the boy Marcel who'd carried me there, Eloise couldn't have been too many years older than I was, yet she seemed to enjoy mothering me. But then, Flore had, too.

"Since you were unconscious when Marcel and Abelard brought you here," she said, "you must have no idea where you are. This is Master Abelard's room on the Rue des Chantres, where he rents lodgings, although he moved here only two weeks ago. The house belongs to my uncle, Canon Fulbert of Notre Dame." She touched my face with a cloth to catch a few drops of milk that had spilled.

"Master Abelard . . ." Her face grew a bit pink. "Since he moved here, he's agreed to teach me. As a student." Her words came a little faster now while she dipped the spoon into the dwindling bread and milk.

"The truth is, my uncle Fulbert has always been very good to me because he has no children of his own. First he had me educated at the Convent of Argenteuil, and now he's decided that I should become the most learned woman in all of Europe. Although . . . some people say that I already am." She gave a modest little laugh as she set down the bowl.

"But—even so, it's—really—" Lowering her head, she said, "Both my uncle and I were amazed that Master Abelard should be willing to teach me. You can't know this, little Spider, since you're not a Parisian, but Abelard is the most famous teacher in the city. In all of France, for that matter. The best dialectician, the most beloved by his students—why, they flock to him from every corner of Europe. They idolize him! Everyone says he's without a doubt the greatest philosopher since Aristotle."

I had no idea who Aristotle was. Or what "philosopher" meant. But from her expression I could tell that Eloise idolized Abelard as much as the others did.

"There, you've finished it all—can you sit up now?" she asked me.

I tried to, but my head spun and I fell back onto the bed.

"Well, you won't be allowed to spend the night in Master Abelard's bed. He sleeps alone," she said as her cheeks grew even pinker. "There's a little closet right at the head of the stairs; I'll fix a pallet for you to lie there tonight."

She crossed the room. At the door she turned one

more time and asked, "Do you understand what a privilege it is to serve him? To be near him? It's like—being allowed to see the face of God."

How strange, I thought, that a woman as magnificent as Eloise should feel so humble toward *anyone*. She was already the most educated woman in Europe—she admitted that. And she must surely be one of the most beautiful. Yet she chattered and blushed like a little girl when she talked about Abelard. What had happened to that proud woman I had first seen in the cathedral? The one who hadn't even glanced in Abelard's direction, who had so coolly kept her eyes straight ahead on the altar, ignoring Abelard and everyone else.

I was so ignorant then about the ways of men and women. I'd heard the songs sung, but the words "in love" meant nothing to me. What I'd witnessed between my mother and father could never be called love: brutality and force on my father's part, and on my mother's part, misery and submission. At the end, she'd escaped him by dying.

In spite of all that had happened to me, I came to them that day as unworldly as a newly hatched chick. But how quickly I was going to learn what love could mean!

CHAPTER SEVEN

Very soon, I became strong again. Not only because I'd been freed from my iron shell, not only because I ate everything they gave me, but because just being near Abelard was like growing toward a bright sun.

Not that he noticed me very often. Abelard was always too absorbed in his own thoughts and actions to care about much else. But he was kind when he explained why he needed me as a servant. I could do other small tasks if I decided I wanted to, he said; that was up to me. My main duty would be to sit outside his door whenever Eloise was in the room studying with him. If I saw anyone start to come up the stairway, I was supposed to knock on the door, and keep knocking until I heard an answering knock from inside the room. That would be the signal that he'd heard my warning.

"Can I count on you for this?" he asked me.

He could have counted on me to walk over hot coals.

At first, I didn't know why he needed me to stand guard. And that only proves how simple I was, because everyone else in Paris seemed to know what was going on. The students had already begun to sing about it in the streets and in the taverns. Whenever I left the house, I would hear those love songs. Slowly, after many days, it began to dawn on me that the songs they were singing were all about Abelard and Eloise.

That left only one person who didn't know: Eloise's uncle, Canon Fulbert. For seven whole, long, incredible months he continued to believe that Abelard was teaching philosophy to Eloise.

It wasn't exactly that Canon Fulbert was a stupid man; there were certain reasons for him to be so trusting. Up until then, both Abelard and Eloise had led pure lives. Even in the bawdy, rowdy student taverns, Abelard's reputation for chastity had stayed untarnished—until he moved into Fulbert's house. And the girl, Eloise, who'd been educated in a convent, had always been cited as a model of virtue.

But, locked together alone for hours in a room— who would have expected anything else? The two of them turned into Adam and Eve in Paradise, devouring the forbidden fruit. They were the perfect man and the perfect woman, and no one came around to interrupt them. Temptation dangled like an apple, within easy reach, too hard for Eloise and Abelard to resist.

Their love had already begun by the time I started keeping watch at the top of the stairs. I'm not ashamed to admit I sat there that first day with my ear pressed against the door, because I was so eager to hear them talk about learned things. I had the foolish notion that if I listened hard, I might become educated, too. All those words in all those books intrigued me. I couldn't read them, but perhaps if I overheard Abelard instructing Eloise about them, I could begin to understand.

Instead, the sounds I heard behind the door were not words from books. Human sounds, but not words at all. I was puzzled.

Living in a tiny hut for the first twelve years of my life, I'd been awakened often enough at night by the grunts of my father having his way with my mother. She never cried out in pleasure—only in pain.

This was different. As I listened from the hallway, I heard all sorts of sounds, and not just from Abelard, but from Eloise, too. And even to my inexperienced ears, those moans had nothing to do with pain. It didn't take me too many days to sense the truth. What I kept hearing, as I grew more and more astonished by their boldness, was a violent, untamed, equally shared lust between a man and a woman.

The storms of passion unleashed in that room were like an onslaught of fire and wind. They came together and made a blaze so ferocious, it would light up the whole world before it devoured itself.

And through it all, Canon Fulbert never suspected a thing.

He was an odd little man. He behaved like a fawning beggar grabbing at crumbs, hoping to pluck a bit of glory from Abelard's fame.

I wondered how he could be uncle to Eloise, because she was all the things he was not: beautiful, brilliant, and unafraid. Canon Fulbert acted more like a shopkeeper than a scholar.

Although I took my meals in the kitchen with the other two servants, I could hear the talk in the main room.

"You were saying, Abelard . . . ," Canon Fulbert would begin.

"What? I've forgotten. What was I saying?"

"About the question of universals . . ."

"Oh. Why don't you ask your niece? She understands the problem as well as I do."

"But—but," Canon Fulbert would stutter, "I'd prefer to hear your explanation."

And in the kitchen, Fulbert's manservant, Pepin, would whisper to the cook, "Abelard thinks he's too good to waste words on Fulbert—eh? And Fulbert lets him live here at half the rent he could get from some other boarder. And most of the time Abelard doesn't even bother to pay."

Neither Pepin nor Nicolette, the cook, worried about me overhearing their talk. Like most people, they assumed that if I couldn't speak, I must not be able to understand, either.

Nicolette answered, "But Abelard teaches the young girl her letters, Pepin. That's worth something."

"Worth what?" Pepin sneered. "A woman doesn't need to know anything except how to tumble in the—"

"Hold your tongue!" Nicolette warned, throwing a glance my way. Maybe she had some notion, after all, that I understood a bit of what was said between them.

"And I think he's already taught that part of it to Eloise," Pepin continued.

Nicolette just shook her head and murmured, "Poor Master Fulbert. Poor, poor, foolish man."

Abelard lectured to two classes every day at the Cloister School of Notre Dame. I began to carry his books for him, which meant I could sit in a corner, unnoticed, while he tutored the hundreds of young men who filled the classroom and spilled over onto the stairs.

To me, everything he said sounded as if it came from the mouth of God. But as the months passed and winter arrived, the students became disgruntled.

"Master Abelard," Joachim called out one morning, "you're talking about the same things you taught us a month ago."

"So? Did you learn it so perfectly then that it doesn't need repeating?"

"But, Master . . ." Several of the other students joined in. "You haven't lectured on anything new for weeks."

"And you never stay after class anymore."

"I had a question yesterday, but you were gone even before the sand ran out of the hourglass."

They grumbled louder among themselves, complaining that Abelard had grown careless, too often repeating old lectures they'd all heard before. If he didn't go back to his former way of teaching, they said, they'd stop coming to his lectures. They'd find a new teacher.

Abelard didn't care. As I scrambled after him to carry his books back to the room, he showed that only one thing mattered to him: to reach Eloise and the warmth of her as quickly as possible.

His classes did not get smaller; the drama of their love affair, which was the talk of Paris, drew students to Abelard now as much as his brilliant lecturing had drawn them before. The students were making bets— how long could Abelard and Eloise keep at it before Canon Fulbert found out? As Fulbert walked to the cloister, his cape billowing behind him in the winter winds, he must have noticed how the students pointed at him and made gestures behind his back. I didn't know how he could stay so blind.

Spring arrived, and the chestnut trees blossomed

long before any other flowers poked up from the earth. By then, Abelard and Eloise had become so sure they were invincible that they would leave the door halfway open to let the spring breezes blow over their skin, even when they lay together in bed. They knew I was always on guard, and they knew I never looked in at them. Even though I'd just turned thirteen, I had little interest in the antics of men and women.

"Spider, come here," Abelard called out one afternoon.

As I entered the room, I was struck once again by their incredible physical beauty. She lay close to him, her dark hair spread out across his bare shoulder, her cheeks warm and flushed, her eyes half closed, her fingers entwined in his blond hair.

He raised his head to tell me, "Look on the table, Spider. There should be a gold coin lying there. Take it and go to the marketplace. My lady has a yearning for wild strawberries." He bent to kiss her, then added, "It may be too early for strawberries, but see if you can find them anyway, Spider. And bring back a flagon of honey mead, and on your way upstairs when you come back, pick up a couple of goblets. And, oh—get violets, too. Buy her as many violets as you can carry." This time his kisses lingered over her open lips. Even though he'd just spoken to me, to him I'd turned invisible once again.

I stood rooted to the floor, unmoving.

"What's the matter with you?" he asked, glancing up. "I told you what I want you to do."

"He's afraid to leave us unguarded," Eloise murmured.

I nodded. That was exactly what I feared.

"Don't worry," Abelard told me. "As soon as you've gone, I'll get up and latch the door from the inside. It's midafternoon, and everyone else in the house is asleep, anyway."

With misgiving, I picked up the coin, scrambled down the three flights of stairs, and went out onto the street. The day was windy, and I pulled my cloak tight around me. Since I'd become servant to Master Abelard, I'd had good, sturdy clothes and shoes to wear: a tunic the color of crushed mulberries, brown leggings, and a hooded cloak as gray as the Seine looked that afternoon, with no sun to catch the little waves the wind whipped up.

I crossed the bridge to the right bank, where most of the vendors had their shops. In my search for strawberries, I tried one stall after another. The best I could find was dried cherries; I bought them and stuffed them into my rucksack. A flagon of honey mead was easy enough to locate, and when I pointed to the violets a flower girl was holding, a whole cluster of flower girls rushed up to surround me, offering their bouquets. "Buy her as many violets as you can carry," Abelard had told me. I bought all they had.

With the honey mead in my rucksack and my

arms full of violets, I hurried back toward the Rue des Chantres. The closer I got, the louder I heard students shouting until I turned the corner and saw—

Books all over the street, their torn pages floating in the wind as laughing, raucous students leaped to catch them. High up, Canon Fulbert leaned out of Abelard's window, screaming in rage while he ripped pages and threw them into the street. Stunned, I dropped the violets; they got blown into the chaos of torn pages and yelling students. Running into the house, I leaped up the stairs three at a time.

Abelard had wrapped his cloak around the naked Eloise, who stood barefoot on the wood-plank floor. Wearing only his bright green leggings, Abelard moved cautiously, one small step at a time, toward Fulbert. The man was hanging halfway out the window now, dropping whole armloads of books into the street. I knew why Abelard was being cautious: One wrong move, and Fulbert could have fallen out the window and been killed.

When he turned around to grab more books, Abelard lunged forward and locked the man into a tight hold. Fulbert's face was bright red, twisted with rage, and dripping with his own spittle.

"Don't hurt him," Eloise begged, but otherwise she stayed as still as a marble statue, her face just as pale. "He's only an old man, Abelard."

"I'm trying not to hurt him." Then, "Give me your cloak!" Abelard ordered me. When I did, he wrapped it around Fulbert and tied it with a belt so that Fulbert couldn't move his arms. The old canon babbled with rage, clenching and unclenching his hands like the claws of a dying chicken.

"Go, Abelard, get away from here as fast as you can," Eloise told him.

"I won't leave you here with this madman!"

"Please, do what I ask. Go away. I can handle this. Send Pepin up here, and Nicolette, too."

From the street rose shouts so loud that hundreds of students must have gathered below by then. "A-be-lard! El-o-ise! A-be-lard!" They were cheering!

Fulbert turned purple, his eyes red-rimmed and bulging like a lunatic's.

I ran down the steps to get Pepin and Nicolette, wondering why they hadn't come up when they'd heard the racket outside. Both of them were sound asleep in the kitchen. After I shook them awake and pointed, they scrambled to their feet. "So it finally happened," Nicolette gasped as she ran, picking up her skirts with one hand and hefting a heavy pan in another. If she planned to use the pan as a weapon, I'm not sure who she thought she needed to hit.

By the time we reached the upper room, Abelard had tied Canon Fulbert tightly to a chair, and Eloise was fully clothed. "Come on," Abelard said to me. "Carry the rest of the books. We're leaving."

CHAPTER EIGHT

ONCE THE STUDENTS LEARNED that Abelard had moved into the Maison du Poirier, they brought back all the books they'd salvaged after Fulbert's outraged frenzy of destruction. For weeks I could hardly cross the room without stepping over the legs of one student or another who sat on the floor, repairing damaged books and sewing together torn parchment manuscripts.

Abelard never slept, it seemed. He began working like a man possessed, writing passages to explain the works of Origen, of Aristotle, Porphyry, Boethius, and all the other philosophers whose names I was beginning to recognize from listening to his lectures. Sometimes he would stop writing and talk to me as if I could comprehend:

"You see, Spider, let's take one individual—we'll

choose Socrates. There is something particular about him that makes him Socrates, and not anyone else. But if we disregard what makes him unique, then we're free to consider simply the man he is, that is, the rational and mortal animal, and at that point we move on to the species. . . ."

And I would nod, trying to look wise, even though I knew my listening meant nothing more to him than a pair of ears to practice his arguments on.

At night he would walk up and down the Rue des Chantres, gazing up at the second floor of Fulbert's house, hoping Eloise would come to the window. Once or twice she managed it, but she was constantly guarded by Fulbert and his manservant, Pepin. Until one afternoon, when by some act of stealth she was able to slip away from her watchdogs.

Abelard had returned from his afternoon class. As always, he sat at his table totally absorbed in his work, writing a gloss on the edges of a manuscript. When the door opened, he heard the rattling of the latch, but he didn't look up. "Yes?" he said absently.

I stood perfectly still, waiting for the moment when he would notice her. Softly, she entered the room.

It was spring outside the window, but the full glory of the season came into the room with Eloise, as though the scent of roses and the breath of fresh breezes swept around her skirts.

"Yes?" Abelard said again, sounding irritated. "Who is it?" And then he saw her.

They leaped together in an embrace, their faces glowing like a thousand candles in the cathedral. It was as though their separation had melted away everything coarse from their passion, and what remained was the pure flame of love.

With her arms raised around Abelard's neck, Eloise's cloak fell to the floor, and the long sleeves of her gown dropped backward to show her bare arms. They were full of bruises.

"What has he done to you?" Abelard cried, his voice sounding strangled.

"It's nothing."

"Nothing! He's beaten you, hasn't he?"

"Abelard, please, you look like you want to kill him. Think how much he's suffered, too. Please, my love, sit down. I have to talk to you before they come searching for me."

Reluctantly, he sank onto a narrow-backed chair.

She stood before him, her hands clasped in front of her, and began, "I'm not afraid of being hurt. Not for myself. The pain of being apart from you is so much worse than anything my uncle could do to me that I hardly notice the bruises. I understand his fury—I betrayed him."

"We both did," Abelard answered, speaking low.

"But . . . I'm afraid for the child."

Abelard grew as still as death. "Child?"

"I'm pregnant, Abelard."

He dropped his head into his hands, but not

before both of us had seen the misery in his face.

Eloise rushed across the room to pull his hands away, forcing him to look at her. "Don't! Oh, don't!" she begged. "I'm—I'm *radiantly* happy to be carrying your child. I only need a safe place to stay until it's born."

For once Abelard, the great orator, was speechless. After a long silence in which his eyes never left her face, as though he needed to carefully memorize every one of her features, he got up and told her, "Wait here. Don't leave this place until I come back. Spider, stay with her and keep out anyone who tries to enter this room. As soon as I'm gone, bar the door."

"Where are you going?" she asked him.

"I'm not sure." He left then, without even looking back.

I did everything he'd ordered, even adding wood to the fire, although the evening was warm. I remembered how cold my mother had always felt when she was expecting a child. Eloise didn't notice me; she paced back and forth across the room, murmuring, "I shouldn't have told him. I could have handled it all myself. Why burden him? It has to be kept secret—it could ruin his future."

An hour passed, and she kept pacing until I, too, was tied up in knots of anxiety. I poured wine into a goblet, thinking she might sit down and drink it to calm herself, but she waved me away. Through the window, which had been left open to catch the sweet smells of spring, I could see that the sky had darkened.

At last we heard his tread on the stairs, and I ran to slide open the bolt. "Thank God my students are fond of me," he said as he burst into the room, smiling. "Do you remember Marcel? Young Marcel DuChesne from Rambouillet? The one who carried Spider to your uncle's house? He'll be here very soon with horses. Spider, gather up my clothes, but not the academic robes. Leave them here. And no books—Marcel will send them later."

"Send them—where?" Eloise asked.

"To my family in Brittany. Where else? You can't bring any of your things, Eloise, but once we reach my father's manor, my sister, Denise, will find clothes for you."

"Abelard, what about your lectures? Your students?"

"If I fell into the Seine and drowned, they'd get along without me, wouldn't they? Anyway, it's nearly the end of the term. Spider, fetch the lady something to eat before we start. Some ham, and sausage." He was speaking so rapidly, I could hardly keep up with his thoughts. "Here's money, Spider—go to the vendors down the street; we don't have time for you to run to the better shops along the quays. Eloise, why are you crying?"

She shook her head, and put her arms around him again. "Believe me, I didn't want to—"

"Save your tears for childbirth," he told her. "As soon as it's full darkness we'll start out so we can leave Paris before the city gates are shut for the night. We'll travel on horseback until dawn and then sleep in a haystack somewhere. Smile, Eloise! It's an adventure. I've been called a wandering scholar—it's about time I took up wandering again."

When Marcel DuChesne arrived, he handed a bundle of clothes through the door to Abelard, who gave them to Eloise. "Here's a nun's habit," Abelard explained, "although God only knows how Marcel got it." He raised his eyebrows at Marcel and said, "You can explain later; I'll be interested to hear." Still talking rapidly, he told Eloise, "These will make us good, simple disguises—I'll take off my academic robes, and you'll put on the habit of a nun." Both he and Marcel laughed at that, as though all this were nothing more than a lighthearted frolic they could later write songs about.

Eloise, though, was taking it seriously. Her dark eyes looked shadowed, and she didn't smile. But she said nothing as she pulled the nun's habit over her dress and hid her dark hair beneath a wimple.

Below, on the cobbled street, the men spoke quietly so that no one in the rooms above would notice anything unusual. "You tied padding around the horses' hooves, Marcel—that was a smart thing to do."

"To muffle the sound. Hooves striking cobblestones make too much noise," Marcel whispered back. "Shall I help you lift Mistress Eloise? Here we go. Up, my lady."

Sitting sideways on a cushion behind Abelard's saddle, Eloise would ride pillion, as women usually did, except for the rough peasant women on farms who rode horses astride, like men.

"Spider, you climb onto the packhorse," Marcel told me. "He's a gentle one, not like the stallion I brought for Master Abelard." The tall stallion snorted, moved sideways, and stomped the cobblestones. It was lucky his hooves had been muffled. Eloise kept her seat and balanced gracefully as the horse shifted when Abelard mounted.

"I'll follow you to the city gate to make sure there's no trouble," Marcel said softly. "I've told some of the other fellows to hang around there until we see that you're safely on the road."

"How many of them? I don't want to attract attention," Abelard said.

"They know that, Master. They'll be careful."

We reached the gate just before the watchman started to close it for the night. "Who are you?" the man demanded.

"I'm a physician returning this nun to her convent at Argenteuil," Abelard stated. "Let us through, man. We're later than we should be. We'll be riding till midnight."

The watchman didn't bother to ask who I might be, trailing behind them. Just another inconsequential servant, hardly worth questioning. Past the gate, Abelard stopped to wave his thanks to young Marcel, who for the rest of his life would tell the tale of this night to his friends.

"Safe travels," Marcel wished us. When he turned around to go back into the city, I saw half a dozen dark shapes melt out of the shadows to join him. Those wild, good-hearted students would all head straight to the taverns now, for a night of drinking and roistering and singing about the escapades of their hero, Abelard.

And then Paris lay behind us. The palfrey I rode was gentle enough that I half dozed while it paced through the dark trees that lined the road. Their branches nearly met overhead, hiding the moonlight. Ahead of me, Eloise's shadow fused with Abelard's as she leaned against his back.

I knew wolves lurked in those woods, but it was the end of May, and plenty of small animals had emerged from their winter dens to provide feasts for hungry predators. We'd be safe. I allowed myself to fall asleep, rocking on the back of the packhorse.

The sky was pink when Abelard halted the horses. "Here's a farmer's field with dry-looking hay. We'll eat now, and sleep some," he said. Sliding off the horse, he helped Eloise to dismount.

I remembered the way my mother had looked in the beginning of her pregnancies: wan, pinched, pale, and sick. I expected the same of Eloise, who'd just spent a long night riding pillion on the back of a horse. But she looked radiant. She laughed as she fell into Abelard's arms. Her cheeks were pinker than the morning-tinged clouds above us.

"How much longer do we have to ride only when it's dark?" she asked him.

"No longer. We'll sleep a few hours, start out this afternoon, and perhaps stay at a monastery guest-house tonight."

"Oh no, my love, let's sleep in the open every night," she pleaded. "It's glorious out here in the countryside. Judging from the bulging saddlebags on Spider's horse, we have all the food we need, and we can buy milk at any farmhouse we pass."

And that's what we did. Early the next morning, after we washed our hands and faces with dew and broke our fast with hard-crusted bread and hard-boiled hens' eggs, Abelard set Eloise on the pack-horse. "Spider can walk for a while," he said. "We'll ride slowly at first."

"Look at us," Eloise said. "The three of us are like the Holy Family fleeing to Egypt, seeking refuge."

In a sense, we were, I suppose. But the biblical image didn't fit us very long. Not much later, Eloise and Abelard left me holding the horses while they went alone into the thickness of the woods. They came back after an hour with their fingers twined together and flowers braided in their hair.

That night, we bedded down beside a brook in

the forest. In the darkness, their voices grew intimate.

"Tell me all about your home, where we're going," Eloise asked him. "And your family."

"It's a small estate called Le Pallet, east of Nantes, about halfway between Nantes and the castle of Clisson. My father's name was Berengar. He owed allegiance to the count of Brittany, but when all of us were grown, he took himself off to a monastery, planning to devote what was left of his life to God. And my mother, Lucia, entered a convent, at the same time and for the same reason."

"Are they . . . ?"

"Father died a bit more than a year ago. Mother still lives in a small, comfortable convent where she prays for me daily."

I heard leaves rustle beneath her; she must have turned toward him to ask, "You're the oldest son— why didn't you stay to be lord of the estate?"

"Hmmmm—it's because I prized books more than land."

I'd already considered Abelard among the noblest of men; when he said that, my awe knew no bounds. Most men spent their lives fighting each other to win more land. Or they married women who inherited vast estates. Yet Abelard cared nothing about what other men grasped at hardest.

He went on, "Learning has always been the only thing I wanted, until I first saw you, Eloise. In my youth I could never get enough of dialectic, grammar, rhetoric, theology—everything but mathematics," he admitted. "Mathematics are my downfall. I can't add up sums to save my soul."

"I can," she said. "And I studied Euclid."

"How impressive." Gently mocking, he murmured, "Did you realize that's why I fell in love with you, Eloise? Because you know Euclid?" Their laughter mingled, soft and low. After a while he went on, "My father was a warrior, but he'd had a bit of schooling himself and he wanted his sons to be tutored even more than he was."

"And his daughters?" she asked.

"My sister, Denise, is the only daughter, and she showed no interest. I was the best learner in the family. Father felt so proud that I was quick—he'd stand me up in front of his friends when I was only seven or eight and make me explain really obscure passages from Scripture."

Sighing, I remembered when I was seven or eight. My own father always hid me out of sight when anyone wandered near our pasture. The fact that he'd fathered a mute, or as he called me, an idiot, filled him with shame.

"When I told my father," Abelard continued, "that I wanted to be a scholar rather than a knight, he agreed wholeheartedly. My brother, Ralph, liked the idea, too, because it meant Ralph would take over the estate and inherit my birthright."

Eloise said, "I never knew either of my parents,

and I had no brothers or sisters. Only Uncle Fulbert."

"Forget him. You'll be part of my family now."

They talked longer, but their voices grew dim as I drifted off to sleep beneath the stars.

CHAPTER NINE

IT WAS THE HAPPIEST TIME of my life.

Our summer in Brittany was moistened by sea breezes that blew in from the coast, not far away. Abelard's sister, Denise, loved to tend her garden, spreading seaweed over the furrows to enrich the soil, while her three small children tumbled over one another like puppies. Her husband, Hugh, oversaw the working of the fields from sunup to sunset. His skin turned the darkest brown I'd ever seen on a man, making the paleness of his blue eyes seem startling.

Eloise reveled in it. She splashed in the duck pond with Denise's children, or threw them up into the haystacks and caught them as they slid down, squealing with glee. The apron she wore over her skirts hid her roundness as the baby grew inside her.

Denise couldn't have been kinder to all of us. She

79

never questioned, at least not in my hearing, why her brother Abelard should suddenly show up on her doorstep with a woman and a mute servant. Denise didn't much resemble Abelard: She was round, red-cheeked, and had a full, deep bosom that made her look as though she'd be more than willing to mother anyone and everyone who crossed her path.

Her husband, Hugh, had not been born to the nobility: He'd been a steward on a nearby estate before they married. Ralph, Denise's and Abelard's brother—always away on some knightly errand or other—was glad enough to leave their estate under the capable management of Hugh.

So all of us were happy, well fed, and merry that summer—all except Abelard. He was restless. Head down, hands clasped behind him, he would pace back and forth in the large hearth room as though he were a prisoner in a cell. He couldn't talk to Hugh because Hugh knew nothing about dialectic or theology or anything else that interested Abelard. Perhaps he and Eloise might have spoken about learned subjects at night, but during the days, she seemed to forget that she was the most educated woman in Europe. All she cared about during those first warm, fragrant weeks were the children rolling underfoot, the bread baking on the hearth, and the vegetables pushing up through the soil.

Yet Abelard's discontent didn't escape her notice. "You need something to do," she told him. "Why don't you teach Spider to read?"

"Read? He can't even talk! How could he read?"

"He doesn't need to say words out loud to read them. Your sister's children are too young to learn, and the peasant children on the estate don't want to, even if their parents could spare them from work. But you're a teacher, so go ahead and teach! Instructing a mute boy would be interesting, wouldn't it?"

I held my breath. I wanted so much to be able to read, I was afraid to even raise my eyes—in fact, I squeezed them tightly shut, waiting for him to speak.

"All right." He sighed. "We'll start with some words he knows by heart—the Our Father." He unrolled an old, scarred piece of parchment. "This is what I first learned on, Spider, when I was three."

Patiently, he pointed out each faded line of the prayer. "Here's the letter 'P.' *'Pater'* starts with a 'P.' The next letter is an 'A.' Point to the 'A.'"

It was as though I'd spent my whole thirteen years waiting for that summer. For hours each day he worked with me. And I learned. Not to write, not to speak, but to read.

Latin is such an easy language to sound out. In only a few weeks I could look at the syllables on the page and say them silently in my head. The problem was that most of the time I didn't know their meanings, because by then, Abelard had begun to instruct me from his own much more difficult books, the ones Marcel had sent from Paris.

"Here's an interesting passage written by Anselm

of Canterbury," he might say. "Listen to this, Spider: *'Vaca aliquando Deo, et requiesce aliquantulum in eo. Intra in cubiculum mentis tuae; exclude omnia praeter Deum, et quae te juvent ad quaerendum eum, et, clauso ostio, quare eum.'* Now, I'll read the words aloud again and you point to them with your finger as I say them, so I can be sure that you really recognize them." Half the time he knew the words by heart. "'Have leisure for God, and rest a while in Him. Enter into the chamber of your mind; banish everything except God and the things that will help you search for Him, and, closing the doors, seek Him.'"

But I had no need to seek, because I had already found my god. And I was living inside my own miracle. Who could have believed that a poor, mute shepherd boy would be tutored by the most famous teacher in Europe?

At night when the others were asleep I sat by the fire to pore over those books, studying, memorizing, feeling blessed to be under the same roof as my personal god, Abelard. For three full months, as the crops grew in the fields, my mind grew just as rampantly, filling up with written words.

Then it was hay-cutting time, and the sun blazed hot. Abelard came into the fields to help, carrying a scythe, but he swung it so awkwardly that Hugh sent him away before he wounded himself or someone else. Next he showed up in the kitchen.

Frowning in exasperation, Denise was too polite to

shoo her brother away, although he got in the way of the servant girls, who nearly tripped over him. Denise bore all this patiently, until Abelard's restlessness gave way to gloom. That was harder for all of us to bear.

He stopped pacing, stopped fidgeting, stopped getting in everyone's way. Instead, he stayed by himself, hour after hour, deep in thought, not talking to anyone.

I would bring one of his books outside to where he sat beneath a tree or beside the duck pond, and place the book next to him. If he noticed it at all, he made no move to pick it up. That meant my reading lessons had ended. If he'd ever bothered to glance my way, he'd have seen bitter disappointment in my face, but he didn't look up.

Eloise and Denise talked about him when he couldn't hear them, using low voices so that I didn't overhear, either. I knew they were worried. Finally Denise, as practical as ever, came up with a suggestion she hoped might pull him out of his malaise.

One evening as they sat at table—at Le Pallet I always helped with the serving, so I heard all that was said—Denise mentioned, "Pregnancy seems to agree with Eloise. Don't you think so, Hugh?" Taken by surprise, her husband grunted and nodded.

"I've never seen a woman carry a child so well," Denise went on. "Eloise is strong, healthy, and in good spirits." Reaching over, she patted Eloise's cheek. "Isn't she, Abelard?"

"What? Oh, yes," he answered, pushing a bit of meat around his plate with a knife.

"Abelard, look at me," Denise ordered him, and the usually gentle Denise pounded the table with her fist. "I'm trying to hold a conversation with you. I think a little travel might be nice for Eloise, and for you, too. Both of you."

Dropping his knife, Abelard asked, "Travel? Where?"

"She's never seen any part of Brittany except here at our estate. You should take her to the sea—salt air's good for expectant mothers. And even better, you should show her the menhirs at Carnac. Take Spider with you to serve you."

"The menhirs are three days' ride from here," Abelard protested.

"She traveled a week when you came here from Paris."

"She wasn't as pregnant then!"

"Let me answer for myself!" Eloise broke in. "First, what are menhirs?"

"Huge stones." Denise was growing excited over her own bright idea. "They're all in a line—hundreds of them. People say giants must have hauled them there and stood them up on end, because they're much too heavy for ordinary humans to move."

"And the dolmen, too," Abelard added, showing a little animation for the first time in many days. "Dolmens are tombs made from the same enormous stone slabs. But three days' ride, Denise—it might not be good for her."

"Of course it would," Eloise broke in. "If I get tired we can stop, can't we? We'll take food and blankets—Spider can bring everything that's needed on the packhorse. I won't ride pillion behind you, Abelard; I'll borrow Denise's mare."

So it was settled, without much more objection from Abelard. I think it didn't matter to him whether he brooded beside the duck pond at Le Pallet or on the road to someplace else.

We started out on a blazing autumn day in mid-September. The trees had become tinged with color, and the smell of ripened fruit hung in the air. From the beginning, Abelard and Eloise kept quite a distance in front of me, while I trailed behind with the much slower packhorse, sometimes riding him and other times leading him. Often I lost sight of the two of them up ahead, but then I'd find them sitting on a fallen log or beside a stream, deep in talk. By the time we built a fire the first night and settled beneath the trees to sleep, Abelard seemed a bit more at peace with himself.

On the second day he told us, "Now we're entering the forest of Brocéliande, the home of the ancient Celts. It spreads over more than half the countryside. Long ago, Eloise, even before the Celts arrived here, this whole land was called Amorica. Then the Celts came and changed the name to Breton, and finally it became Brittany. And to confuse things even more, across the sea from us lies the land of Britain, which is another name for England."

"Are you descended from Celts, Abelard?" Eloise asked.

"I suspect so, since they were wild rebels who detested authority." Turning to me, he said, "Have you ever heard of the sorcerer Merlin, Spider? They say he was born in this forest. And that he's still here somewhere, trapped inside a prison built of layers of air." Thoughtful again, he said, "Brocéliande Forest is supposed to be enchanted. A place of magic and mystery where, if you make a wish, it might come true."

His words, spoken in that low, serious voice, were enough to make the murky forest even more mysterious for me. Mystical, too, especially when he added, "I suppose all three of us—you, Eloise, and I, and even Spider—carry wishes deep inside us that we'd like to have come true."

There in Brocéliande, beech and oak trees grew so close together that the sun stayed hidden most of the time. Vines twisted and twined among holly bushes, while clumps of mistletoe grew high and hung down from the branches of the giant oaks. I shivered a little, but not from fear. From excitement. The idea of riding through a place of enchantment pleased me. As long as I stayed near Abelard, I had nothing to be afraid of, I thought then.

By the third day we broke free of the dark forest

and rode into the sunlight. Ahead, far in the distance, I saw the menhirs.

No matter what Abelard had said about them, nothing could have prepared me for the sight of them: hundreds of enormous stones, each taller than a man, and some as tall as two or three men standing on each other's shoulders. In parallel rows, they lined up from east to west like a massive army waiting to be ordered into battle.

"Who could have put them there?" Eloise asked in wonder.

"Not nature. Not God," Abelard answered. "Men. And women, too, probably. But not the Celts—these stones were here long before the Celts arrived."

Eloise drummed the flanks of her tall mare with her heels and, gripping the saddle horn, galloped wildly off toward the menhirs. Abelard caught her mood. Laughing more loudly than I'd heard him in a month, he spurred his horse to follow her. They left me in the dust, plodding along behind them with the placid packhorse.

When I reached them, they'd dismounted and were running in circles like unruly children, snaking back and forth around the huge menhirs until both of them fell exhausted to the ground. They sat there, backs against one of the huge stones, catching their breaths while I tied all three horses to bushes to let them graze.

Abelard was no longer melancholy. Now the look

in his eyes was even more disturbing: Headstrong. Reckless. Stirred up and ready to take risks.

He pulled Eloise hard against him and told her, "You and I are alike. I wouldn't be surprised if both of us descended from the same wild Celtic tribe. Celtic women were ferocious—they worked with their men and fought side by side in wars with them. The women probably killed more enemies than the men did. I can imagine you, Eloise, standing beside me to lop off enemy heads." He caressed her cheek with the back of his hand.

Seizing his hand, she kissed it, then pulled him to his feet. "Come, show me the dolmen," she said.

I headed toward the horses but he told me, "No, Spider, leave them. We'll walk. You come, too."

We wound our way through the rows of menhirs, whose shadows and ours all pointed in the same direction: toward the dolmen. As we walked, Abelard said, "I've been told that across the Channel, in England, massive rocks like these are found at a place called Stonehenge. But the Stonehenge rocks form a circle, while on this side of the Channel, our menhirs all stand in rows. Yet the same people must have put them up, and for the same reasons, whatever they were."

We reached the dolmen. It was built of enormous slabs of rock, some reaching straight up, others balanced on top of the upright slabs to make a roof.

"Legend says this is the burial place of a powerful

pagan chieftain," Abelard told us. "My father brought me here when I was a little boy. Don't worry, we can go inside—if the rocks haven't collapsed since I first came here all those years ago, they won't fall down on us today."

Within the dolmen, in spite of the gloom from shadows, narrow shafts of brilliant sunlight shone down through spaces in the roof. "It's a funeral chamber," Abelard said. "But it isn't only about death, it's about birth, too. And fertility."

He pointed to a wall, where one massive slab had been carved into the shape of a woman's torso. Clearly, it was meant to show a womb swollen with child. Eloise touched it, gingerly at first. Then, sweeping her hands in circles, she rubbed her palms over the damp surface of the bulging rock. After that she wiped the moisture from the carving onto her own face and arms and abdomen. Even in the shadows, I could see that her eyes had grown large as she asked Abelard, "What else do you know about the magic here?"

"They say"—he took her face between his hands—"that if a person sprinkles holy water over the menhirs outside, a violent storm will be unleashed."

"Let's try it," she said softly. "Only we don't have any holy water."

Abelard's answering laugh, low and bitter, sent shivers through me. "My mother told me she dreamed

I was a priest. If her dream was a prophecy, I should be able to turn ordinary water into holy water, shouldn't I? Give me the flagon, Spider."

I handed it to him. Holding it high overhead in his left hand, he raised his right to make the sign of the cross, chanting, *"In nomine Patris, et Filii, et Spiritu Sanctus* — I proclaim this water to be holy."

They ran together out of the dolmen, hand in hand. Tearing around the menhirs as though they'd lost their senses, they dashed water onto one giant stone after the other, and then onto each other. My breath stopped at their boldness. What they were doing seemed too close to sacrilege! I made the sign of the cross.

"Let the storm come!" Abelard shouted. "Do we fear it, Eloise?"

"No! Never! If we're not afraid to love each other without the blessing of the Church—"

"Then we're not afraid of pagan superstition!"

"Or anything else! Oh, my love!" She fell into his arms, and they clung to each other, spinning around and around on the yellow autumn grass as though they were drunk, although they hadn't had a drop of wine.

When Abelard looked up and saw me frowning at them, he laughed and said, "Bring the food, Spider. We'll feast like wild Celts here in this pagan place. Everything we touch will be enchanted."

After spreading out Abelard's cloak, they lay side

by side on the ground as I served them—bread with honey; cheese and apples; plovers' eggs flavored with thyme. They plucked grapes and placed them into each other's waiting lips, not noticing that the sky overhead had turned the color of tarnished brass. Salty sea air blew around us, lifting Eloise's dark hair from her shoulders and whipping it in long strands across Abelard's face.

"Leave us," he told me. "Don't bother cleaning up the food—just go. We need to be alone."

The fields stood open for miles around, except for the giant menhirs that guarded the plain like ancient warriors. I walked back to the dolmen and went inside it once more, just in time to escape the first raindrops.

Crouching on the packed earth, I circled my knees with my arms, feeling small. Wind whistled around and through the giant slabs that formed the dolmen. Just after the first streak of lightning, just before the first rumble of thunder, I felt the hair on my arms stand up. I thought I'd found safe shelter there from the storm, hidden inside the womb of the earth. Instead, I began to sense a strangeness around me.

My head filled with the sound a seashell makes, held against the ear. When a bolt of lightning illuminated the inside of the dolmen, it lit up carvings and runes I hadn't noticed before. A place of magic, Abelard had said.

A place to make a wish.

I couldn't say it aloud, but in my heart was a wish that had been inside me for most of my life, growing larger and larger as the past year had unfolded. Silently, in this place that might be enchanted, I made the wish.

If there is magic here, let my tongue be set free. I want to speak like Master Abelard. I want to be like him.

Still clutching my knees to my chest, I focused all my consciousness inward, and held my breath. I believed I could feel the magic happening. It covered my skin like warm water, dripping down inside my chest, fingering my throat like loving hands. Saliva filled my mouth. In that ancient tomb, I knew I was swimming in magic.

Opening my lips, I prepared to at last break the spell that had held my tongue prisoner since birth. Which words should I say? Here in the tomb of a pagan, my first spoken words ought to praise Christ, I decided. *In nomine Patris.* In the name of the Father, and the Son . . .

For the first time in almost ten years, I would hear the sound of my own voice. I knew it was going to happen! I clutched my shoulders in anticipation.

"Aaaah naah aaah!" Animal sounds came out of my mouth, the way they had when I was three years old and my father had beaten me almost senseless for trying to talk. They were the same grotesque noises

I'd made then, like a sheep being butchered. Nothing had changed. I clamped my lips shut and bit them savagely with my teeth, enraged at my own stupidity. What made me think I deserved a sorcerer's magic? Or a miracle from Christ, either? I was beyond curing. I would never speak.

Full of despair, I left the shelter of the dolmen. The storm began whipping rain sideways in brutal sheets, filling the path between the menhirs with water. Where were Abelard and Eloise? Running all the way, I found them just where I had left them, but now they were standing instead of lying down, with the rain pouring hard over their heads. It flattened their hair into wet ropes that clung to their faces.

To be heard above the thunder, Abelard shouted, "I have to go back to Paris. Do you understand? I can't stay in Brittany. It's as though I've died inside. I have to go back."

"I *want* you to go back," she answered. She may have been weeping, but if she was, her tears melted into the rain. "You belong in Paris. You need the company of ideas."

"Will you come with me?" he asked.

"I'll stay with Denise. After the baby is born — we'll see."

"Perhaps it's better that way," he said.

"Yes. Better." But the pain in her eyes gave lie to those words.

Tears from all three of us watered the plain of

Carnac that day, joining the streams of mud that surged around the menhirs and carried all our wishes into emptiness. If the place was supposed to be magic, it was a magic like Merlin's that set everything backward.

CHAPTER TEN

THEY DECIDED THAT I SHOULD STAY with Eloise in Le Pallet. With the birth of the baby only a few months away, she needed a servant more than Abelard would. That decision didn't make me too sorry: After Abelard left, I felt a bit of sadness— yes—but also a bit of relief. As much as I missed his company, I was glad to escape his moodiness.

The weather turned cold, and to pass the time, Eloise took over my reading lessons. She was an even better teacher than Abelard, with much more patience. She seemed to sense when I couldn't understand a passage, and would explain its meaning in ways I could more easily grasp, then go over it again and again until I comprehended it.

"I wish I knew what you thought about this philosopher's opinion, Spider," she said one day in

November. "I know you have no voice, but have you ever tried to shape words with your lips? If you could, I'd look closely at your mouth and perhaps I'd be able to make out some words. Then you could express to me what you're thinking. Will you try?"

And Eloise leaned close to me, her eyes focusing on my lips. She wanted to know what *I thought!* No one had ever cared before what I thought. Her nearness addled me so much that I could do nothing except open and close my mouth like a gaping fish. Even if I'd been able to shape words, my brain had emptied completely of whatever thoughts might have been lurking there, if any. The blood mounted into my cheeks.

"It's all right," she said, and gave me a quick hug. "What we need is for you to learn to write, because that way you can express yourself. Tomorrow I'll begin to teach you to write."

But it didn't happen. The next day Abelard's brother, Ralph, rode onto the estate with half a dozen of his men-at-arms. My lessons came to an end. So many extra men in the house meant considerably more food needed to be cooked and served, and benches had to be set up at night for beds. The men slept beneath fur skins on leather sacks stuffed with straw. Each morning, all that had to be cleared away.

The men and their dogs tracked mud across the floor; it needed constant sweeping up. And I was kept busy chasing those hunting dogs, who came bounding into the house and trying to leap onto the tables every time the door opened. Ralph's men were good-natured, but boisterous and careless. Still, the estate belonged to Ralph. He had the right to bring as many men there as he wished.

He was surprised to find Eloise living with Denise and Hugh, but he treated her with courtesy, even giving her a gift. "It's English wool," he said, tossing a sackful onto the floor at her feet. "The finest wool in the world. Much better than that grown here in Brittany. English merchants are getting rich trading it all over Europe."

I knelt to open the sack and took out handfuls of the fleece. What Ralph said was true: It was far better wool than any I'd ever held before. The fibers were thick, yet soft, too.

Eloise thanked Ralph warmly, saying, "I only wish I knew how to spin. Spinning wasn't the sort of thing they taught me at the convent."

I hurried to one of the dusty outbuildings and came back with a distaff and a drop spindle I'd noticed there months before. Sitting on a stool next to Eloise's feet, I grasped a handful of the wool and began to spin.

"Look!" she cried in delight. "Our Spider is spinning. I didn't know he could do that."

"All spiders spin—how else would they make webs?" Ralph asked, and let loose a great guffaw of laughter over his own joke. He was a big man, broad-shouldered and loud, not at all like his brother, Peter Abelard. He seemed the same kind of person as their sister, Denise, with a happy nature and a generous spirit.

"So with your Spider spinning for you," Ralph told Eloise, "you'll have enough to make a blanket for the expected child."

Denise lifted some of the thread from my spindle and held it close to the candle flame to examine it. "No blanket with this," she declared. "It's much too fine to have a baby spit milk all over it, not to mention the other things babies do to whatever they're wrapped in. If Spider can spin the whole sackful of wool into thread this good, we'll make a cloak for Eloise. She needs one. Winter's here, and she had to leave all her clothes behind when she fled Paris."

Ralph looked interested as he heard, for the first time, that Eloise had "fled" Paris. He was too chivalrous to ask about it in front of her, but I knew that as soon as he was alone with Denise, he'd demand to hear the full story.

The weeks stretched into and through the season of Advent. Soon the baby would be born. Abelard had promised to return for the birth, but it was getting close to Christmas and he still hadn't arrived.

"He'll come," Eloise said with confidence. "He said he would spend Christmas with us. Travel must be hard at this time of year. Something could have delayed him."

But there was nothing under heaven or earth that could delay the birth of the baby when it decided to arrive. Three days before Christmas I was chased out of the house, along with all the other men. We took refuge in the barn alongside the cows and pigs and chickens. It was warm enough; body heat from the animals and moisture from their breaths kept us comfortable as we sat close together, lounging on cut hay.

"If it turns into a long birthing, we may spend Christmas Eve in here," Ralph told his companions and his brother-in-law, Hugh. "Which would be fitting enough."

"More fitting would be to spend Christmas Eve in the stable," Hugh answered. "The Christ child was born in a stable." He wiped his mouth with his sleeve, then offered his flagon of honey mead to the others.

"Except, what's happening inside isn't exactly a holy birth," one of Ralph's men-at-arms said. "That woman in there is bearing your brother's bastard—"

Ralph leaped to his feet and grabbed the man by the throat. "Watch your tongue or I'll cut it out," he growled. "The newborn will be my nephew." Dropping the man onto the straw, he added, "Or perhaps my niece. Either way, it's my brother's child, so it will be part of our family, the same as Hugh's and Denise's children."

"That's right," Hugh agreed. "Like one of ours. No different! All the same."

Just then one of the serving girls pulled open the

barn door to fetch me. "Spider," she called out, "you're wanted in the house."

I was wanted. Not the others, who stayed outside warming themselves with the mead.

They led me to the bed where Eloise lay holding a baby in her arms. Truly, she looked like the Madonna, with her face all tender and smiling.

"Since his father isn't here, I wanted you to be the first man to see him," she told me. "After all, you were there, on the other side of the door, when he was conceived."

She'd called me a man! No one had ever called me that before. I still looked like a boy—a very young boy, in fact. I hadn't stretched out much more than two inches since . . . since they'd welded the metal shell around my shoulders and my groin at Master Galien's house of grotesqueries. Inside me, though, I believed that I'd grown toward manhood, because in the past year and a half I'd learned so much. Eloise must have known that when she called me a man.

Bending over the bed, I peered at her son. I'd been the first to lay eyes on many newborn infants in my mother's arms, but never one as fine and healthy as this. Gently, I reached out, wanting to touch him but afraid to because my hands were dirty from the barn, and he looked so new and clean.

She said, "I've chosen a name for him. First, 'Peter,' for his father, and then 'Astrolabe.' Peter Astrolabe."

I nodded, although I thought it was an odd name for a boy. Peering closer, I saw that he had the sturdiness of Denise and Ralph, not the fine-grained, scholarly features of his father or his mother. Peter Astrolabe wore the look of earth about him, not the look of the stars he was named for.

As promised, Master Peter Abelard arrived in time for Christmas. As he sat on the bed doting over the two of them, watching Eloise nurse the baby, he stroked both their cheeks with his long, thin fingers. I thought once again of the Holy Family, and this time, the image lasted. But not long enough.

He spent only a week with us, and then it was time for him to return to his lectures in Paris. "You must stay here with little Peter Astrolabe," he told Eloise. "It wouldn't be safe for either of you to travel for a week on the back of a horse in this cold weather. And keep Spider to help you. I'll come back for all of you at Easter."

She sighed deeply, but didn't argue with him. "Until Easter, then," she said.

This gave me three more months to study, on my own and as well as I could, the works of the great philosophers of ancient times. Mostly I read at night, by firelight, while all the others were asleep. Although I understood no more than a tenth of what I read, I was grateful that I could understand any of it. This was the world of ideas. I'd come from a world of things: sheep, wool, spindles, grass, hungry bellies.

The world of ideas was infinitely more exciting.

Eloise was too busy with the baby to spare any time to teach me further, but she allowed me to use her books, so I struggled through them on my own. During the days, while she cared for little Astrolabe, I would sit spinning until all the wool from England had been turned into fine yarn. Denise and Eloise, together, dyed the yarn a warm brown, using walnut husks to give it color.

When the blizzards of February came, we sat by the fire all day, weaving. Denise had found a hand loom in the same outbuilding where I'd picked up the drop spindle. She taught us to weave—both Eloise and me—and we took turns working on the cloth that would become a warm, hooded cloak.

And then it was Holy Week. I had my fourteenth birthday, which no one knew about. Even though the birthday was my own secret, I did receive a gift—the return of Master Abelard.

As always, when Abelard burst into the manor house, the place came alive with energy. The serving maids smiled more and bustled faster, putting plates on the table and taking them away; Ralph and his men told stories far into the night, sitting around the fire, drinking and bragging about the fights they'd been in; even baby Peter Astrolabe waved his arms, smiling and drooling whenever his father came near his cradle. And Eloise radiated happiness.

On the third night, after we'd celebrated the

Easter feast, while the remains of pastry and roast lamb and dried apricots still littered the table, Abelard stood up to announce, "Fill the cups! I have something to tell all of you."

Everyone, even the servants, gathered around the hearth. Abelard caught Eloise around the waist and pulled her to him.

"Since last harvest," he began, "I've lived alone in Paris without the woman I love. For a good reason— her uncle hated me for stealing her from him, and he was right to hate me. I did him a great wrong, accepting his hospitality under his roof and then . . . then . . ."

"It wasn't all your fault, Abelard," Eloise broke in. "I was just as guilty."

"Yes. Guilt. And the guilt has weighed heavily on me," he told us. "Also, I was afraid that Fulbert would hurt Eloise in some way if I brought her back to Paris."

Denise nodded; she'd seen the bruises on Eloise's arms when she'd first arrived.

"But then the season of Lent came, time for me to rid my soul of guilt in order to prepare for the feast of the risen Christ. And I did it!" He raised his cup. "I've made peace with Fulbert. Now Eloise can return to Paris."

"How . . . ?" she began, frowning.

"I told him I would make you my wife!"

Cheers broke out from everyone in the room, and the serving girls hurried to pour more wine into each cup. But I was watching Eloise, and what I saw on her face stopped me from any thoughts of rejoicing.

"No!" she cried sharply. "I will not marry you!"

Abelard laughed and pulled her closer. "Don't joke, Eloise. Your uncle Fulbert is the happiest man in Paris now. We have nothing more to fear from him."

"Abelard, you can't marry! Scholars aren't supposed to marry. It will ruin any chance you have to advance."

The smile left Abelard's lips as he realized she meant what she was saying. "That doesn't matter," he claimed.

"Of course it matters! No one cares if you have a mistress, and that's what I'll continue to be—gladly! I'd rather be mistress to *you* than wife to the king! But if you marry, no one will take you seriously as a scholar."

Hugh scratched his head. "This makes no sense," he said. "Why should marrying be bad for a scholar?"

"I think it started back with Aristotle and Plato, didn't it?" Ralph asked. "A scholar should devote his life to learning, they believed then, and I guess they still believe it now. A scholar is supposed to be above fleshly desires, even if he isn't a priest."

"Yes, exactly!" Eloise answered, a fire in her eyes. "They're calling Abelard the new Aristotle, and they hold him in the highest respect you can imagine because he's so brilliant in what he writes and teaches. But if we marry, he'll be scorned. Marriage would bring him down to the level of ordinary men, with common, earthly cares—babies and servants and a house that reeks of cooking." Turning to us, she held out her hands as if beseeching us to understand as she tried to explain. "They'll forgive him his lust— half the canons at the cathedral have women they keep in secret. But they won't forgive a marriage."

"That's crazy!" Denise objected.

"It's the way the Church looks at things, and the Church controls all advancement, even when a man isn't a priest. How can Abelard stand on the shoulders of the giant philosophers, they'll ask, if his attention is pulled earthward by the needs of a family?"

Abelard's jaw worked. He wore that same look of defiance I'd seen when we'd visited the menhirs. "I have given Canon Fulbert my word," he declared. "There's no turning back."

"I won't do it!" Eloise tried to break away from him, but he caught her by the wrist.

Abelard was shouting now. "I said we will marry. And by God, we will marry!"

"Then God help us both," Eloise cried. "Because this marriage will destroy us."

CHAPTER ELEVEN

IT WAS A GLOOMY PROCESSION back to Paris. Abelard looked grim, and Eloise mourned because she had to leave Peter Astrolabe behind, with Denise.

"We'll have him soon enough," Abelard told her. "A while after we're married, you and Spider can ride back to fetch him. It will seem more proper then to have a child around."

Eloise pulled her hood closer to almost cover her face; she seemed to sink inside the cloak. We'd had no time to finish the brown cloak properly. It reached only a little below her knees, but it kept her warm because it was woven so tightly.

The cold was not in the air; it was between the two of them. They hardly spoke. When we were only one day's ride from Paris, Abelard spurred his horse in a fury and galloped far ahead of us.

"Let him go, then," Eloise muttered. "Since he won't listen to reason, let him go."

But he came back in a quarter hour, riding toward us at a deliberate pace, pulling back on the reins so that his stallion lifted its forelegs high, as though prancing in a parade.

"All right," Abelard shouted even before he reached us. "I've thought of a compromise. We'll keep the marriage a secret. If we say our vows before a priest, Fulbert will be satisfied. He won't care that nobody knows we're married, as long as we are, before God."

"You don't know him!" Eloise cried. "When you're my husband, Fulbert will want to shout it from the rooftops. He'll never agree to a secret marriage. He'll take pride in being connected by wedlock to the famous Abelard, and he'll want the whole world to hear about it."

"What do you know about men's pride—you're a woman! I say Fulbert cares mostly about getting satisfaction for the way I wronged him."

"Hah! You're a fool, Abelard." This time it was Eloise who spurred her horse to ride ahead.

But as always, Abelard had his way. They were married, supposedly in secret, in a small chapel with only Fulbert and his manservant, Pepin, as witnesses. And me—I was there, too, in a corner, as inconspicuous as ever. And as sharp-eyed, because I noticed everything.

While the priest said the words of the marriage

service, I studied the faces of those in the chapel. The priest himself was secretly excited because he was uniting, in marriage, the two most famous people in Paris. Abelard had sworn the man to silence, but I could tell it wouldn't take much wine to loosen that priest's tongue.

Fulbert looked like a man who'd been given the keys to a treasury. His eyes glittered—with more than just satisfaction over justice finally coming to him. He was reveling in his triumph, like a man who'd vanquished his enemy and was about to rake in the spoils from the battlefield.

Eloise, the bride, looked sorrowful. She wore a simple dark gown, and kept pressing her arms against the front of her sore breasts. It had been only a short time since her baby was taken from her, and she was suffering pain, both physical and emotional.

As for Abelard—he wore the expression of someone who'd demanded his own way and gotten it, but who'd begun to wonder now whether he'd made a mistake. For a wedding, there was not much joy inside that chapel.

Of the two servants present, Pepin's lip curled with contempt whenever he glanced toward Abelard, and I felt heavy with foreboding, especially when Eloise went home with her uncle Fulbert. The bride and groom didn't have even a moment together to toast each other with wine.

Not much changed in the weeks that followed.

Abelard and Eloise continued to meet secretly, as though they weren't even married. There I was, standing guard outside the door of a married couple, the same way I had when they were illicit lovers. From the sounds that came from inside the room, their passion hadn't cooled down, not one small bit. Maybe it had blazed up even stronger, fueled by the strangeness of their marriage. When they did come together, they could never seem to get enough of one another.

As for me, I had a passion of my own—learning. Now I was allowed to attend all of Abelard's lectures, and even better—I understood them! Or at least some of them. At night I sat by his fire and read the books he'd taught from during the day. And I carried the parchments to the table he wrote on, and brought him ink and pens and fine sand to blot the ink with, and when he finished writing and went to bed, I would stand above the table with a candle, reading the new things he'd written that day.

But aside from my joy over what I was learning, it was not a happy time for any of us.

"I'm afraid of him, Abelard," Eloise said one evening as she was leaving to go back to Fulbert's house.

"Has he touched you?" Abelard demanded.

"No. But he's growing angrier each day because he can't brag about our marriage. He wants everyone to know that you're his kin. I see the rage in his face. He can barely keep it from showing, no matter how hard he tries to hide it from me."

Abelard rubbed his tonsure, that clean-shaven spot on his head that was supposed to be the mark of his celibacy. "I don't like any of this. If Fulbert's rage breaks loose, he could harm you. I think I'd better take you to the convent at Argenteuil for a while. You'll be safe there with the nuns while I decide what I can do to calm Fulbert."

"Shall I leave Paris disguised as a nun again?" she asked, trying to sound lighthearted, although I could see that she dreaded another separation.

"Why not? It worked the last time."

They left me behind. This time they didn't need a servant to follow with a packhorse, since the convent was only a few hours' ride away. And I think they wanted to be alone, to draw out the trip as long as possible so that for once they could spend a few uninterrupted days and nights together.

So I was the one who felt the full fury of Fulbert's rage. The long sleeves of his black robe flapped like the wings of an avenging vulture as he came flying up the stairs to Abelard's room. "Where is he? Where is he?" he shrieked. "He'd better be here! He's not in his classroom, and I can't find my niece, either. Someone said they'd ridden out of Paris together, with Eloise dressed as a *nun!* That had better not be true."

He tore around the room like a lunatic, flinging books onto the floor, pulling clothes out of the chest as though Abelard might be hiding inside it.

"You imbecile!" he screamed at me. "Abelard chose a servant who couldn't talk, did he, so you can't answer my questions?" He picked me up and shook me until my teeth rattled. Although Fulbert was a small man, and growing old, his fury gave him strength. He threw me onto the floor. When I scrambled under the table for safety, he ran after me and knocked over the table.

Kicking me, he shouted, "Is it true he's taken her to the convent?"

Frightened, I nodded, because I didn't think revealing that could hurt Abelard or Eloise in any way. It seemed innocent enough. But I didn't understand how Fulbert's mind had already been twisted beyond reason by his hatred of Abelard.

"He's going to have the marriage annulled!" he screamed. "He's going to make her take a nun's vows so he can be a priest, isn't he? Because he wants to be pope some day! That's it, isn't it?"

I shook my head vehemently, but the man was far past the boundaries of common sense. "He lied to me! He's having the marriage annulled! He's making her a nun!" All the way down the stairs, stumbling, falling from side to side and catching himself against the walls, he kept shrieking. I ran across the room and bolted the door, because I didn't want him to come back. If Canon Fulbert wasn't all the way mad, he was verging on madness.

After I put the room to order again, picking up

the table and books, folding the clothes back into the chest, I found a piece of parchment on the floor. Fulbert had torn it from one of the manuscripts; it looked as though it was beyond mending.

I lit the candle, sat at Abelard's table, and for the first and last time in my life, tried to write.

If only I'd learned how, that time when Eloise had promised to teach me! But I'd never before held a pen in my hand. I dipped the point into ink, then pressed it against the bit of torn parchment. Too hard! Ink splattered over half the space I had to write on.

I tried again, printing the letter "B." Or what was supposed to look like a "B." After an hour, I'd only succeeded in filling the small piece of parchment with illegible ink blots.

I turned it over to the clean side. All night I labored over that note, going as slowly as possible, trying to control my hand, which had started to shake from the unaccustomed position. Anyone else could have spoken aloud to warn Abelard, but I had no voice. And there was no other witness to Fulbert's madness except myself. I wanted to tell about Fulbert's crazy suspicion that Abelard planned to annul the marriage and become a priest, but I never could manage to convey all that. The best I could do was try to write a warning. Finally I managed to put down two words I thought Abelard could make out: "Beware Fulbert."

When he came back, a few days later, and saw my

note, he assured me that Fulbert couldn't harm Eloise. "I've told the nuns at Argenteuil that if he goes there, they must not let him in. There's a strong wall around the convent and a strong gate in the wall—that will keep him out."

I shook my head and pointed to Abelard.

"What? Me? He can't hurt me—he's an old man. Still, if it will make you feel better, Spider, you can take a blanket and sleep at the bottom of the stairs for a few nights. If he should come around, just bang on the wall."

It sounded simple. It would have been, if Fulbert had come alone. But many nights later, when the hours of darkness had almost given way to the approaching dawn, he came with Pepin.

I'd been asleep. It happened fast—Pepin grabbed my arms and wrenched them behind my back, snarling, "No need to stopper his mouth—the dummy can't talk."

That could have been my one chance to sound the alarm. If I'd tried to yell—even if I'd made those wretched butchered-sheep noises I'd choked out in the dolmen—I might have saved Abelard. But I was too used to my own silence to think about croaking a warning, and I only had a few seconds. Then it was too late.

"Just to be safe . . . ," Fulbert muttered, whipping out a scarf. I thought he was going to strangle me, but instead he used it to gag my mouth. They left me there, bound, trussed, and muzzled, as they stole quietly up the stairs.

How did they get past the bolt on the door? I never knew. But Abelard was always careless about locking doors. I heard him screaming. Why didn't anyone else hear him and come to his aid? Frantically I clawed the ropes that tied my wrists, and managed to loosen them just as Fulbert and Pepin stomped down the steps, not bothering this time to tread quietly. At the door to the street, Fulbert stopped. Holding a bloody knife in his hand, he leaned forward and cut off the scarf he'd tied around my mouth.

"Imbecile!" he spat at me, and then they were gone.

Master Abelard was alive. He had to be, because I heard him moaning. Afterward I didn't remember how I'd gotten the rest of the ropes off my legs and raced up the stairs to his room.

Inside, it looked like a slaughterhouse—blood splattered all over the room. Abelard lay across the bed, naked from the waist down. When I saw what they'd done to him, I gasped.

He'd been mutilated! Like a stallion turned into a gelding, like a bull turned into a steer, they'd cut away his manhood. It looked as though he'd tried to defend himself with his knife, but they'd come on him too quickly; the knife lay where it had been flung—on the floor at the bottom of the bed.

Roaring with pain, Abelard dragged himself off

the bed to pick up the knife. Now he was the one who looked insane. As I stood there shaking with horror at what they'd done to him, I was too dumbstruck to save myself.

Knife upraised, he lunged at me. Instinctively I tried to scream, but no sound came out. With his strong left hand he clutched my throat, pulling down my jaw and clamping his thumb around my back teeth so that I couldn't close my mouth. And then he thrust the knife blade at me. I lurched; it caught me under my tongue.

Spitting blood, terrified, I ran from the room and never looked back. A fountain of blood spewed out of my mouth, smearing the walls as I ran downstairs.

The sun had just risen, lighting the streets barely enough to see. Only a few students were out and about, getting an early start so they'd have the front seats at Abelard's lecture.

"Look!" one of them cried. "Isn't that Master Abelard's servant? He's covered with blood."

"God! What could have happened?" another shouted. "Quick! Get up to Master Abelard's room. Maybe Fulbert murdered him!"

Abelard wasn't dead. Neither was I. But neither of us would ever be the same again.

CHAPTER TWELVE

W HERE COULD I GO? Not back to Abelard's room!
He hadn't killed me the first time, but he might if he
tried it again. And who would blame him? It had
been my duty to guard him against Fulbert, and I
might have done that if I'd been alert enough. Even
after Pepin grabbed me, I could have let out some
kind of a yell, but the habit of all those years when I'd
refused to make a sound had doomed both of us.

Until nightfall I cowered under the bridge, vom-
iting blood. I had nothing to eat and nothing to drink,
yet I couldn't have put anything into my mouth if I'd
wanted to. My pain was close to unbearable. But
when I began to groan, I stopped myself with the
thought of the worse pain Abelard must be enduring.

He wouldn't die; I knew that. In my father's pasture, we docked the male lambs every year to make

them docile, because we never needed more than one ram. The lambs bled, but castration never killed them.

Remembering the sheep and the pasture, I knew where I would have to go, because I had no other choice. Nearly two years had passed since I'd seen my father and my brother, Eustace. Would they let me come back?

When night fell, I started on the road to Les Andelys, feeling sicker and sorrier than the prodigal son. My mouth burned like the fires of hell. As I staggered along I realized that sooner or later I'd have to drink—I'd had no water for twenty-four hours. Leaving the road, I wandered through the forest until I came to a brook. Kneeling, I leaned on my hands and lowered my head to the water.

It was like putting hot coals into my mouth. How could cold water burn so hot? Pain made me feel faint; I fell into the brook. I lay there, crying, not just because of my mutilated tongue, but because of all I'd lost. No more learning. No more Eloise. No more Abelard, who'd been my god. He was no longer a god; now he was no longer even a man. And he'd tried to kill me.

After I finally pulled myself out of the water, I lay down on the banks of the creek and slept. The sun came out to dry my clothes, which had been washed almost clean of the bloodstains.

The next days and nights have mercifully been

lost to my memory. Somehow I returned home, and my father found me. God showed me another mercy, too—my brother, Eustace, no longer lived there. It seemed he'd married a farmer's dairymaid and moved to the valley. Heaven help the poor dairymaid, I thought.

It was as though I'd never been gone. My father asked me no questions, since he could hope for no answers from a son who was mute, and—he thought—stupid. I was back, there was work to be done, he expected me to do it, and that's all there was to that.

Alone on the chalk cliffs, I tended the sheep once again, day after day. Slowly, my mouth healed. At first I lived only on milk, because that was all the nourishment I could manage to swallow. Then came the day I decided to try a small bite of cheese.

That was how I learned what had happened to me. Swallowing felt different! With my fingers, I probed the inside of my mouth. It still hurt me sorely, but not as much as it had at first. And I realized—

My tongue was free!

Abelard hadn't been trying to kill me at all! Certainly, if he'd wanted to, he could have plunged the dagger right into my heart. Instead, he'd deliberately cut the cord that had bound my tongue to the floor of my mouth!

Cautious, I made a sound. "Aaa." I swallowed, and tried another. "Be"—and then the hard one—

"lard. Abelard!" It didn't sound right, and another person might not have recognized the name at all, but it was the first word I ever spoke aloud. And no one heard it. Nor would I let anyone hear me speak; not until I'd practiced alone on those chalk cliffs. I determined that I would become a great orator like Abelard, no matter how long it took.

How foolish I was!

I thought it wouldn't be hard. In my head, I could hear words—I could even create, in my memory, the actual sound of Abelard's voice reciting lines from Ovid. I'd memorized those lines. But a person who's been silent for fourteen years doesn't start to talk all at once. Not in a month. Or a year. Or ever, and expect to speak properly.

I practiced for hours, out there on those lonely cliffs. Then I'd grow discouraged. To keep from sinking into despair over my failures, I decided to distract myself with something I was good at.

The flatland on top of the cliffs grew a layer of gorse and broom and other low bushes that the sheep rubbed against while they searched for grass to eat. I began to gather the clumps of wool that caught on the branches of those bushes. Soon I had enough to spin.

Spinning was so easy for me that it didn't occupy my mind, which left me free to fret about the terrible turn my life had taken. So I decided to make something different than I'd ever tried before. A rope.

I spun the wool fibers extremely fine, then wove

them together like a lanyard. Adding strand after strand, layer upon layer, I built the rope to the thickness of my thumb. Over the months, I made it longer and stronger until I believed it could have lifted up a horse.

All that time I was learning to speak, too. Watching the sheep was easy; they hardly ever strayed. So I sat on a boulder, making rope, shouting out poems from Homer, and keeping entirely to myself. No one knew what I could do. Especially not my father.

At night in our shepherd's hut I would spin ordinary yarn, which he would take into Les Andelys and trade for bread and wine. We lived on mutton, sheep's milk cheese, which I made myself, a few vegetables I grew outside the hut, and water—I drank the water, my father drank wine. And he drank it, and drank. More, it seemed, every day.

He began to see things when he was drunk—things that weren't there. "What's that?" he'd cry, his eyes wide with fright as he pointed to an empty wall. "It's a devil! It has cloven hooves. Get away!" And he'd end up screaming at hordes of imaginary devils he said were closing in around him.

God forgive me, I did nothing to help him. Since most of the time he never knew whether I was there or not, I'd leave and go to stand on the edge of the chalk cliffs, where I would sing one of the songs Abelard had composed for Eloise. That way I could drive my father's ravings out of my head.

If I did stay in the hut, likely as not I'd get beaten. It was easy for me to outrun my father now since his leg had never mended properly after he'd broken it, and when he was drunk he'd fall down if he tried to catch me. Sometimes—again, forgive me, God—I would deliberately maneuver around the hut, baiting him to give chase, just waiting for him to fall with a crash, knocking over stools as he fell with his hands reaching out to clutch at me.

One night, though, he staggered after me out to the cliffs. "Where are you, you little piece of entrail?" he raged. It was a full-moon night; he had no trouble finding me. I could have run back to the hut, but I'd grown tired of always being the victim, running away from everyone else's rage or madness or drunken brutality.

My rope had been left coiled at the base of the only thick-trunked tree on top of the cliffs. While my father stumbled around babbling, I tied one end of the rope—which was quite long, now—around the tree trunk, and the other end around my waist.

Then I walked up to within a few arm's lengths of my father, and stood there until his bleary eyes focused on me. "There you are!" he yelled. "I'm going to break your head against these rocks! I'm going to . . ."

His eyes grew wider and wider as I backed away from him and—disappeared!

Now that I think back, I was crazy to trust that rope to hold me, but it did. I should have tried it in daylight first, lowering myself a foot at a time over the edge of the cliff, instead of leaping backward all at once, to dangle over the Seine so far below me, like a spider swaying on a thread of silk.

Above, I could hear my father screeching in fear, "Demon! Where'd he go? He's a fiend—he dropped right back into hell!"

And I laughed out loud, the first time I'd ever had anything to laugh about since I'd found my voice. I liked dangling there off the cliff, hanging by a thread I'd woven myself. Bright moonlight painted the vertical surfaces of the chalk walls the color of cream. From the retreating sound of my father's shouts I could tell he was going back to our hut, where he'd no doubt fall down in a stupor. I'd stay where I was until that happened.

Testing the rope, I swung back and forth, from side to side. Then I pushed backward with my feet, but that was too dangerous because momentum pulled me back against the face of the cliff. If the rope had broken, I'd have been dead, since the Seine lay so far below that all I could see of it was moonlight reflecting on the water. But right then I felt invincible. I thought of all the things I'd learned to do— read, sing, laugh out loud, weave a rope strong enough to hold my weight above the silent, black, midnight waters beneath me.

No longer was I an ignorant, mute, and timid peasant boy. I had served the most famous philosopher of the century. I'd been taught by his wife, had rocked his child, had read his creations when the ink was not yet dry on them.

Spring had come again; I'd just turned fifteen years old. As soon as the sheep were shorn and I'd spun enough yarn to let my father buy enough wine to drink himself to death, I would leave Les Andelys.

I would go to find Abelard, who had set me free.

CHAPTER THIRTEEN

I TOOK NOTHING WITH ME except the clothes I'd arrived home in, plus a loaf of bread and my rope. Coiled, it hung over my shoulder.

The season was autumn, the month September, the day almost exactly like the one when I'd first traveled to Paris three years earlier. Nothing on the route seemed changed. Identical gaggles of geese waddled in front of small boys who drove them with sticks. The same creaking carts rolled by, full of pumpkins or turnips or cabbages. The people, as always, laughed, gossiped, and quarreled while they trudged through the dust of the road. And I stayed just as silent as I had those three years before. I'd made a vow that the first person to hear me speak would be Abelard.

At night, when the other travelers bedded down

not far from the roadside, I forged deeper into the forest, searching for solitude to practice my speech.

It was all thought out carefully in my head, but I needed to rehearse it so it would be perfect. When I reached a place deep enough in the woods that I couldn't be overheard, I knelt, just as I planned to kneel before Abelard. Raising my hands in supplication, I practiced the words I would say to him:

"Master Abelard, I wronged you. I was not a worthy servant, because I didn't keep those evil men from attacking you. But if you let me serve you again, I promise that for the rest of my life I'll devote my every breath, my every action, to your safety and well-being."

Fine words, but when I said them out loud they didn't sound right. My voice was too high and reedy—nothing like the deep, resonant tones that Abelard used. And I still couldn't shape the words properly, not even after a year and more of teaching myself to talk on the lonely chalk cliffs of Les Andelys. I tried so hard to pronounce the phrases like other people did, but I couldn't make them come out in a way that satisfied me: Too many words were garbled, or lisped, or slurred. For two whole years I'd had the good fortune to listen to the greatest orator in the world, so I knew how words *could* sound. How they *ought to* sound. If only I could say them that way!

The second night in the forest, I rehearsed even longer, feeling gloomier every time I repeated the speech. Master Abelard had cut my tongue loose so that I could talk. But to speak nicely, in a way that wouldn't grate on people's ears or annoy them and humiliate myself, required certain mechanics of tongue and throat that I seemed to lack. It didn't matter how hard I tried.

Discouraged, I slept in the woods. At sunrise I started out again. With each step that brought me closer to Paris, my confidence dropped.

Shaking with apprehension, I climbed the steps to the room where I'd last seen him. Blood smears still stained the stairwell walls—my own blood, I supposed. No one had bothered to clean it.

At the top of the stairs, the door stood open. The room was empty. No bed, no table, no chest, no sign of life. It had the stale smell of a room that hadn't been lived in for months.

Next I went to his classroom in the cathedral cloister, but it, too, was empty. By then it was late afternoon. I had no place to stay, but that didn't bother me—hunger did. Food required money, and I had none, but I knew how to get some.

I went to the banks of the Seine, where dozens of barges floated, tied to the quays. During the time I'd served Master Abelard, I'd learned how to bargain with tradespeople even though I'd never said a word. Now I could haggle out loud if I wanted to, but— keeping to my vow not to speak until I'd found Master Abelard—I decided to barter the way I always had. Silently. Anyway, tradespeople usually got so disconcerted by my silence that I ended up getting the best of every bargain.

The first boatman I showed my rope to asked, "Where'd you get this? I never saw a rope like this before." He yanked at it. "Stronger than . . ." His eyes narrowed; if he praised the rope too much, he'd have to offer more. "Three sous," he said. I coiled the rope again and walked along the quay to the next barge.

"Wait!" the first boatman called out, following me, but by then the second boatman was examining my rope. "Five sous," he offered, but the first boatman had reached us by then and he said, "Seven."

A small, interesting scene was stirring up there alongside the river, as I knew it would. More and more bargemen came to see what was happening and why the first two boatmen were shouting at each other. When the newcomers caught sight of my rope, they began bidding, too. No one had ever before seen a long, strong rope made entirely of wool, woven like a lanyard, with one layer above another of fine, tight strands. After a quarter of an hour I walked away with eighteen silver sous, enough to feed me for weeks.

By then the beautiful, rose-petal sky reminded me that it was evening and I was in Paris, and before long the taverns would fill with students. It was in those taverns that I could find out what had happened to Abelard.

"Look! It's Spider! He's back." The students remembered me, and peppered me with questions. "Where did you go? We thought you'd died—they said you were bleeding like a slaughtered calf. Were you there when Fulbert—?"

"Leave him alone. He can't talk, remember?"

But the students hardly ever *stopped* talking that night. During the entire course of the evening and far into the morning hours, they spoke about nothing except Master Abelard. Stories about him flowed through the taverns like the wine, pouring out endlessly as the night wore on.

I learned that after his mutilation, Abelard had put on the brown robes and cowl of the Benedictine monks, and had joined the order, taking his solemn vows. At the same time Eloise had taken the veil at Argenteuil. So she really did become a nun, as her uncle Fulbert had feared and predicted. Yet I was sure she didn't want to, and wouldn't have, if Fulbert hadn't destroyed Abelard's manhood.

"His enemies all thought Abelard would be a laughingstock after he'd been gelded," one of the students said. "But that didn't happen."

Another took up the story: "Even after he joined the Benedictines at the Abbey of Saint-Denis, students flocked to hear him lecture. The crowds got bigger and bigger. Then he got into some kind of squabble with the other monks—"

"And . . . and . . ." More students kept trying to

add details to the telling. "We asked him to write a book explaining the Trinity so we could understand it, and he did, but that got him into trouble, too, because they said he shouldn't be teaching theology since he'd never been trained as a theologian—"

"Right! So now they're trying him for heresy! For *heresy!* At Soissons. Can you believe it?"

"It's because they're all jealous of him. Everyone knows that's the reason. They can't stand it that he's so successful, even after what happened to him—when Fulbert cut him—"

They were all shouting at once; I had trouble sorting it out. Close to morning, they spilled out of the tavern onto the street and almost immediately, a young man galloped up to them on horseback.

"Here's Dagobert—he's been in Soissons," they cried. "What's the news?"

"The Council hasn't been able to prove any heresy against Abelard—so far," the rider answered. "But they won't let him speak in front of the Council fathers to defend himself."

"That's no surprise. He'd make his accusers look like fools."

"We need to go there to show our support for Abelard against those—"

"Those pious prigs!"

The students began to shout. "Let's take the road to Soissons! Starting right now. Sois-sons! Sois-sons!" they chanted.

"We can walk there in a few days, can't we?"

"Anyone who doesn't come is a Judas."

That's how I became part of a ragtag band of students on the road to Soissons. The wealthier ones had gone on ahead, riding horseback. The band I was part of consisted of poor, hand-to-mouth youths who loved learning but never knew where their next meal was coming from, not to mention their books or wax tablets to write on. On the road they shared everything: food, cloaks, stories, and songs, especially the songs of romance Abelard had written about Eloise. They would pool whatever money they had (and I contributed part of my carefully hoarded sous) to buy a meal for all of us at a tavern or a parsonage.

At night we bedded down among the blackthorn hedges and hawthorns in the woods, cutting green rushes to lie on. And still they kept talking, half the night through. They loved to talk, those students!

"Dagobert says the worst they can accuse Abelard of is what he taught us—that a man is able to believe only what he has first understood. 'For by doubting we are led to questions, and by questioning we arrive at the truth.' That's what Abelard said."

"Faith needs reason to back it up, he taught us. That's why he's in trouble. The holy fathers don't like us to think."

"Right. And they made him submit his book to the Council for judgment. They're going over it page by page. They want to trap him."

"Which book?"

"The one we're talking about, idiot—*De Unitate et Trinitate Divina*. Of Unity in the Holy Trinity."

"What could they find wrong with that?"

"They had to stretch, but they came up with his argument about the copper seal. They're saying it's heretical."

I knew what that was. I'd heard Abelard lecture on the point before I'd run away to Les Andelys. To teach the idea of the Trinity, he'd compared it to a king's seal. The seal is made of copper; that's its substance, and it represents God the Father. The picture of the king on the seal gives it its form, as in God the Son. God the Holy Ghost, in this analogy, proceeds from the actual act of sealing—the pressing of the king's image into wax—since that arises from both the copper and the image itself. It was the kind of knotty concept that scholars loved to argue, but one that ordinary folks couldn't have cared less about. If that was the worst they could find to accuse Abelard of, he was sure to be declared innocent.

Soissons, when we got there, was full of noisy, quarreling crowds. The debate going on in the Council had spread to the streets, where the townspeople were fighting the outsiders, pushing and shoving students who pushed and shoved right back. Just before it reached the stone-throwing stage, we heard, "Hurry to the cathedral. They're about to announce the verdict."

A thousand wax candles burned inside the cathedral, and dozens of pine-pitch torches hung in sconces on the walls. Thick coils of black smoke curled up from all of them as their flames cast dancing shadows on the high ceiling. Those points of fire, added to the body heat of the thousand or more people packed inside the cathedral, seemed to suck up the air, leaving little of it to breathe. I felt myself growing dizzy.

I never would have seen anything at all if one of the students, a big, ox-muscled fellow, hadn't said, "Here, Spider, sit on my shoulders," and lifted me up high.

From there I could breathe better, and I could see Abelard. He looked strange and different in the brown robe of a Benedictine monk. He stood as still as a graven statue while four men pushed through the crowded cathedral to make a path for a priest carrying a brazier. Small flames licked up from the coals in the brazier, adding to the already hellish appearance from everything else that was burning.

Another priest, holding a book, came up to Abelard. "This is what you wrote," he cried out. "You are commanded to burn this book because it contains heresy."

A howl of protest rose from the students in the cathedral, but Abelard, stone-faced, took his book from the priest's outstretched hands. Holding it out straight in front of him like an offering, he dropped it onto the coals. As the flames curled around the pages, blackening them, the students groaned. Still, Abelard said nothing.

The cathedral grew very quiet as Abelard's book was consumed by flames, so quiet that we could hear the crackling and spitting of the sheepskin parchment when it flared. All those words, consumed by fire! Words he'd spoken aloud to me as he'd written them, trying them out—not for the benefit of my ears, but for his own.

"Listen to this, Spider," he would say back then. "If *'Deus'* and *'divinitas'* have precisely the same meaning, then one might say, using *'Deus,'* that 'God' has suffered. Yet, using *'divinitas,'* wouldn't it be incorrect to say 'divinity' has suffered? Of course it would!"

Words! Even as he'd spoken them in those days, I'd thought how foolish it was for scholars to waste time pricking and poking at words, fretting as they haggled over different ways to use words, arguing hotly about small differences in meaning. What did it matter to common folk like me? It was like mothers picking lice eggs from children's heads—pinching one, squinting at it through narrowed eyes, dropping it to the floor with a look of disgust, grinding it underfoot. All that attention to one little nit, when the child's head teemed with them!

The silence continued until Abelard's book was reduced to ashes. It was broken when one of the priests called out, "I saw what he wrote in those pages—that only God the Father is omnipotent."

"Not true," the students roared. "He never wrote that! We know what he taught us from the book—" And both sides began to quarrel so loudly, the echoes from the rafters made my head ache.

A feeling of revulsion swept over me. Why had I wanted so much to be able to talk? What good was speech? Men used it for wrangling, to pit one man against another, creating bitter enmities over foolishness like this. The cathedral vibrated with angry shouts of "he said," and "he never said," and "the meaning is this—" and "you're a fool!"

Finally the archbishop stood up and struck the stone floor with his crosier, again and again. When some sort of order was restored, he declared, "It would be well for our brother here"—and he pointed to Abelard—"to publicly state, before us all, the faith that is in him."

"Good!" the students muttered, jostling one another and grinning now. "At last they're giving him the chance to speak for himself. Just watch what happens—he'll demolish them."

Abelard, too, looked hopeful, but as he opened his lips, the archbishop commanded, "Brother Abelard, you will prove your faith by reciting the Athanasian Creed."

Immediately a priest strode toward Abelard and unrolled a scroll, holding it up in front of his face.

It was a copy of the creed. Even I knew what an

insult that was. To display the words before Abelard as if he needed to read them because he couldn't remember them, when every schoolboy in the land had memorized those lines by the age of eight!—it was the worst mark of contempt they could have shown him, as if he were totally ignorant of what the Church taught.

But Abelard accepted the humiliation. While tears ran down his cheeks and his voice choked with emotion, he humbly recited the creed:

"'. . . the Catholic Faith is this: That we worship one God in Trinity, and Trinity in Unity . . .

"'But the Godhead of the Father, of the Son, and of the Holy Ghost, is all one, the Glory equal, the Majesty co-eternal. . . .'"

His voice built in volume until it rang out with its usual, familiar power. He finished the lines of the creed, filling the cathedral with sound, never once letting his eyes rest on the page in front of him. Once again I was swept up by the magnificent sound of his voice. It resonated through me like the blood pulsing in my throat.

"They have to release him now," the student holding me said. "After burning his book, after shaming him like a schoolboy, what worse can they do to him?"

But it wasn't over. The Council, speaking together, pronounced his sentence. "Brother Abelard will be placed under house arrest at the Abbey of Saint-Médard!"

The four monks who'd cleared the path for the brazier battled their way through the shouting, angry students and took hold of Abelard. They led him away, out of the cathedral, down the stone steps, and into the street.

"This Council is now dissolved," the archbishop cried out.

Discouraged, disgusted, furious, heartsick, or all of those things together, the students poured out of the cathedral to gather in the streets. For a while it looked as though they might riot, but a retinue of sixty men-at-arms who served the abbot of Saint-Denis restored order by forcing their horses through the crowds. Students who didn't want to be trampled had to get out of the way. After an hour or so, in little groups, they began to drift back toward Paris.

I didn't go with them. If Abelard was going to be held prisoner at the Abbey of Saint-Médard, I'd find my way there. It wasn't hard; the abbey was only a little distance outside Soissons.

I waited at the abbey gate. And waited! Day after day, sitting on the ground, I listened for any bit of gossip about what was going on inside. The poor people who waited at the gate with me had no interest in church disputes, and they probably didn't care two straws about the fate of Abelard. Their only concern was their empty bellies.

Every evening a monk would come to the gate to give food to the beggars gathered there. I never took the food they handed out because I still had a bit of money from the rope, and the poor needed alms more than I did. But I pressed forward each time the gate opened, in the hope of catching a glimpse of Abelard. It never happened.

Waiting outside with nothing to do, I kept remembering those angry voices in the cathedral, the words all twisted in devious tangles to crucify Abelard. What good was a voice used to destroy? I vowed I would never raise my own voice, now that I had one, to deceive anyone. It was not a vow I made to God, because in those few weeks after witnessing the shameful hypocrisy in the cathedral, I was no longer sure how I felt about God. The vow was made to myself.

Then one day, at midmorning, the heavy wooden gate creaked open a few inches and I heard, "Spider! Come here! Quickly!"

I scrambled to my feet to find Abelard peering out through the narrow opening in the gate. "I have only a few minutes," he whispered. "Ah, Spider, what the Council did to me was cruel! Worse than what Fulbert did, when he mutilated those certain parts of my body—I deserved that, because I'd sinned with Eloise. But the Council! When they made me burn my book, that tore the *heart* out of me! Where was the justice? To say that I'd taught false doctrines. . . . Lies! All lies."

And that was how he greeted me after an absence of a year and a half. He didn't say, "Spider, I'm glad to see you. Where have you been? How have you lived? Are you well?" Nothing like that; just a long tirade on the terrible way he'd been wronged by the Council and how much his enemies hated him. Disappointment stung me.

Because of that, even after all my rehearsing of the speech I'd planned to make when I saw him again, it turned out that I said nothing at all.

"I could see you from inside the abbey," he told me. "I've been waiting for the chance to give something to you. Here, take it." He thrust out a bit of parchment. His eyes, peering at me through the crack in the gate, looked a little wild. "Take it!" he commanded. "Look at it! On this side is a single word— you see? 'Rambouillet.' That's where I want you to go. You'll have to find your way there on foot. At each village show this word to the parish priest. Rambouillet. He will direct you how to get there."

I must have appeared as puzzled as I felt.

"Don't you recall? Rambouillet is the estate of Marcel DuChesne," Abelard said irritably. "He inherited it last year. He is now the lord of the castle."

Marcel! I hadn't heard his name spoken in so long, I'd almost forgotten about him. Marcel was the young student who'd carried me from Master Galien's house when I was first freed from my iron shell. The one who brought us horses the night we escaped from Paris and fled to Abelard's family.

"This single word—'Rambouillet'—is what you

show to ask for directions, since you cannot speak."

It seemed Abelard had completely forgotten about cutting loose my tongue with his knife, freeing it so that I could shape words. Perhaps all the terrible things that had happened to him had driven it from his mind. I almost told him then, but before I could open my mouth to get out a sound he said, "I must hurry. Pay attention, Spider! On the other side of this scrap is more writing, see it? It's a message to Marcel, telling him to keep you with him. When I need you again, I'll send for you."

Had it ever occurred to Abelard that someone might not be willing to carry out his orders? What if I didn't want to go to Rambouillet? How did he expect me to stay alive while I got there? I had a few sous inside my belt, but Abelard couldn't know that. And, anyway, what if Marcel objected to keeping me while we both awaited word from Abelard?

No, of course Abelard would never worry about our preferences. He commanded; we obeyed. Even as a virtual prisoner inside the abbey, he ruled us.

"Go now," he said. "To Rambouillet." And the gate creaked shut.

CHAPTER FOURTEEN

BEING INCONSPICUOUS HAS ADVANTAGES. I was able
to walk through the outer gates of Rambouillet by following the cart of a farmer who'd come to pay his rent
with sacks of barley. No one questioned me or
stopped me, so I kept going and slipped inside the
castle. Hugging the shadows, I crept along the outer
hall, searching for Lord Marcel.

As easily as that, I found him. He was lounging in
front of a chessboard, playing the game all by himself.

"Spider, is that you?" he cried, leaping to his feet.
"Where did you come from? Here, sit down! You
look dusty and road-weary and probably famished,
and"—Marcel threw back his head and laughed—
"taller! Finally a little taller than the boy I carried into
Master Abelard's room. But you're just as silent as
you were then."

If I'd wanted, I could have astonished him by speaking, but I decided not to. All the way from Soissons to Rambouillet I'd managed just fine without using any words. Often, silence provided me with more information than words would have. Almost everyone assumed I was deaf as well as mute, and they whispered things that put me on guard, such as, "He has money—he bought bread at Hermione's house. Make a sign to him that he can sleep in the barn, and then we'll rob him." More than once I'd heard such whispers, and each time I'd managed to escape.

Also, since I wasn't sure how Lord Marcel would feel about Abelard's wish that I stay there, I kept quiet as I handed him the scrap of parchment.

"What's this? For me? From Master Abelard? Really?" Enough of the hero-worshiping student remained in Lord Marcel to make his hands shake when he studied the note. "It says you're supposed to live here until he sends for you."

I nodded.

"I'll be more than happy to host you, Spider. Come with me and I'll show you to my wife." As soon as he said that, he hesitated. "No, maybe that should wait until you've had food and drink and a hot bath and some rest."

No doubt I was too smelly and disheveled to meet a fine lady, since I'd spent so many nights in barns or in manure-strewn fields. I let Marcel's servants lead me to the luxury of hot water and clean clothes. After I'd eaten, they took me to a soft bed, where I drifted into a deep sleep that lasted for hours.

Night had fallen when I awoke. I found my way to the same chamber as before, where a dozen candles burned. Lord Marcel still pored over the chessboard. Standing just inside the door, I studied him.

He'd changed. No longer a tall, thin, good-natured youth, he was now a full-grown man, one who'd come into a rich inheritance. He wore a velvet tunic of two different colors, and a heavy gold chain around his neck.

When he noticed me standing there, he said, "Hmmmm, my wife says she'll see you in the morning. Do you play chess, Spider? No? Sit down and I'll teach you. My father brought this set back from the Crusades. See the Arabic design?" He traced the strange marks on the pieces with his finger.

That was the beginning of many hours I would spend leaning over a chessboard, seated across from Marcel. I learned the game quickly, though I never enjoyed it much. To me, games seemed such a waste, a rich man's diversion that poor folk could never afford the time for. But it pleased Marcel to have me play with him, so I tolerated it.

The next morning Lord Marcel led me into a curtained chamber with tapestries, where several women sat idly passing the time. Some were decorating a long altar cloth, embroidering crosses and doves on it.

One was brushing and plaiting the hair of the most beautiful woman in the room.

"This is my wife, Lady Clarisse," Marcel said, leading me to where she sat. Luckily, in my travels I'd learned enough about manners to bow properly before her.

She wore a dress the color of spring lavender, tightly fitted down to her waist and then flaring out to hang in pleats. Even to my unpracticed eye, it looked as though it had cost a great deal of money. And her fingers were heavy with jewels.

"This is Spider, my lady," Marcel introduced me. "I told you about him last night."

"Oh!" She laughed a little. "So now we have two spiders."

Lord Marcel looked sheepish. Turning to me, he muttered, "My father-in-law gave us the other one as a wedding present. I couldn't refuse to accept him. Anyway, the ladies like him."

I didn't know what he was talking about until I heard the strings of a lute being plucked, and I turned around to see—Rabel!

He bowed so low his chin almost touched his knee. "We've already met," he told everyone. "Odd that you should call him Spider. He was nameless when I knew him. He didn't want to be a juggler then, and I suppose he didn't become one. And he most definitely did not want to become a spider."

Astonished, I stumbled backward. Rabel's arms

and legs were even longer than when he'd lived in Master Galien's house. They made his torso appear pinched and distorted—I supposed he was still squeezed inside that iron shell. His eyes were just as colorless, his skin even more pale, but his hair, which had been the lightest blond before, now looked altogether white, like a plant that grew under a rock and never saw the sun.

"Give us a song, Rabel," one of the ladies begged.

"Gladly, my lady." He dropped to his knees before this particular lady, who was so tightly laced into her dress that her bosom swelled above it. First he kissed her hand, then he plucked the strings of his lute and sang:

> "My lady's blush is tender pink,
> When with my kiss her lips are fed,
> Lying with her beneath the trees,
> Upon her breast I lay my head.
> My lady's blush has turned, I think,
> A deeper shade of blood-rose red,
> Tonight I'll beg her, on my knees,
> And she'll invite me to her bed."

My lips twitched with distaste. After having heard the songs Abelard wrote, the ones sung all over the streets of Paris by students, Rabel's tune sounded inane, flat, and badly rhymed. But the ladies seemed enraptured. Their needles had stopped darting in and out of the altar cloth. With their own rosy lips parted, they cried, "Again, Rabel! Please sing another. Another love song."

Lute in hand, he sprawled on the floor with his long legs in front of him and his head on the silken lap of one of the women, who stroked his forehead. Staring up at her with his colorless eyes, he began another silly ditty about love.

I turned away, finding the whole scene a mockery. What did Rabel know about love? He sang songs of romance, but how could he have understood their meaning, raised as he was from boyhood in Galien's house of horrors?

For that matter, what did any of those ladies know about love? All their marriages had been arranged for political or social advantage, sometimes tying them to men older than their own fathers. Hardly any highborn women were allowed to choose their own husbands. No wonder they wanted to hear about fictitious lovers embracing beneath the trees.

Perhaps Lord Marcel loved his wife as much as he needed to, just because she was beautiful. But as I compared her in my mind to the brilliance of Eloise, Marcel's wife seemed as dull as a rock. I stayed in the company of the ladies only as long as I had to to be polite, and then I escaped from the room. If that was the life Galien had planned for me, thank God Abelard had rescued me from the whole sordid business!

In Marcel's castle, I was given a small alcove curtained off from the great hall. It was close to, but not part of, the servants' quarters. My bed was a wide bench piled high with sweet grass and reeds under a fur coverlet. A woolen blanket lay rolled up at the head.

That night as I got ready to sleep, Rabel came to me. "Don't think you're moving in here permanently," he told me. "This is my place. These are my ladies to entertain. One spider is enough here—two are too many."

I shook my head and raised my hand in a pledge to show him that I had no plans to stay at Rambouillet. That seemed to reassure Rabel. With a bound, he landed on my bed.

I could see that he was a little drunk, and more than a little concerned about competition from me. He certainly had no worries on that score. To do what he had to do, day after day, singing insipid songs to those idle women, would have made me wither and die. His colorless brows knit in a frown as he stared at me with those pale, unearthly eyes.

Draping his long arms around his lute, he began, "They say you lived with Abelard and Eloise. Oh, the tales you could tell me if only you could speak. I could make up such wonderful songs about them! But—" He sighed. "Since you can't gossip to me, I'll share my own gossip with you."

His eyes lighted with both mischief and malice.

"Master Galien got more money for me than for any freak he'd ever sold before. What do you think of that?"

I guess I didn't look impressed enough, because he added, "*You* wouldn't have fetched nearly as high a price. I'm worth a lot because not only is my skin as white as an orange blossom, and my eyes the color of parchment, but I have a lovely singing voice, too."

I nodded, already wondering how I could get rid of him.

"The only one who thought *you* were special was Flore. She cried for days after you left because she said you were the one pretty child she'd ever taken care of in Master Galien's house. And then guess what happened!" He gave a great bounce on the bed. "Flore got pregnant!"

My deep astonishment must have shown in my eyes. Rabel giggled with satisfaction.

"Can you imagine—that ugly, twisted old hag? No one knew who the father was. She must have gotten some man so blind drunk he couldn't see her in the dark. I guess some curs will mate with anything." Rabel gave another high-pitched giggle, then went on. "It wasn't Master Galien. He couldn't have been the father—I know that for a fact. Galien preferred a different kind of love." Again, that silly, half-demented giggle.

I no longer wanted him to leave. I wanted him to stay. I was straining at the bit for him to go on with his tale, and he knew it. To torment me, he got off the bed and yawned. "Well, time for sleep. Good night."

Diving at him, I grabbed him around the shoulders and wrestled him to the floor, where I knelt on his chest with one knee. I'd have kept him there all night to make him finish telling what he'd started.

"What's the matter with you? Why are you doing this to me? Could it be—could it possibly be?—that you want to know about Flore? Well, get off me, then, and I'll tell you."

Smirking, he sprang up and dusted off his silken tunic. "She had the baby! Yes! It was tiny, but perfect. And perfectly beautiful. A little girl. Flore stayed with us only a few months after the birth, and then one night she simply disappeared." Rabel rocked on the bed again, cradling his lute like a baby in his arms. "She took the baby with her, of course. I suppose she went off somewhere to work as a cook for a rich man, hoping her daughter will stay pretty and grow up to seduce the rich man's son."

When he said that, I had the urge to grab his lute and hit him over the head with it, but there was no sense harming a perfectly good lute. Instead, I shoved him into the hall. Then I threw myself back onto the bed to think about what he'd told me.

Flore. She'd tried to be kind to me, and I'd rebuffed her. Poor, loveless woman—but loveless no more. Now she had a child of her own to love. All the different patterns love takes, I thought. And yet, none of them had touched me deeply since my mother's death.

I idolized Abelard, but it was mostly a feeling of awe and respect. He was so far my superior that we could never be equals. As for Eloise, I felt the same reverence for her, yet it was easier because she'd treated me like a younger brother, not like a serving lad. But the love the two of them had for each other — that love was so intense, it pushed everyone else outside its consuming circle. They were eagles; the rest of us were wrens.

I wondered if I would go through life without any of the romantic passion Rabel sang about. Yet my life was rich with experience, and I was not unhappy.

Marcel had a tailor make me several tunics and leggings, and a shoemaker fit me for new boots. "So you'll look nice for the ladies," Marcel said, but since I couldn't stand to be stifled in that room with the ladies and Rabel, I took to wandering around the castle's keep by myself.

Marcel was a good man, yet his peasants lived lives as hard as all the other peasants in the rest of the countryside. Their huts were dark and cold and thick with smoke from cooking fires. A quarter of the crops the peasants raised had to be paid to Marcel for rent on the land; in years when crops were poor, the people nearly starved. As I walked around in my fine new clothes, I pitied them because they wore the same ragged tunics all year round, winter and summer, and they stank.

Marcel showed me every courtesy, treating me almost as a guest in his castle, but I disliked leisure, was bored out of my head by the idle chatter of the women, and felt embarrassed to be fed so well while his peasants went hungry. How long would I have to wait until Abelard sent for me? A month went by, and then another. Slowly the seasons changed: summer, autumn, winter. Silently—because no one had any idea that I could talk—I wandered the estate, feeling pampered and useless as I watched the peasants freeze inside their hovels.

It wasn't as if we didn't know what had been happening in Abelard's life. News might travel slowly across France, but it eventually spread to every corner of our land, as well as to Burgundy, Brittany, Provence, Navarre, and all the rest. Pilgrims and priests, merchants and troubadours, all could be sure of a good night's lodging anywhere, as long as they brought news and gossip to share. Since Abelard was the most famous man in France, any tales about him reached us quickly.

We already knew that after his house arrest at the Abbey of Saint-Médard, he'd gone back to the Abbey of Saint-Denis, where he'd caused so much dissention among the monks that they'd banished him to the wilderness. It didn't take students long to find out where he was. They came in droves, turning the wilderness into a village of crudely built thatched huts, a chapel, and an oratory where Abelard taught and preached. He named it the Paraclete. And that's where he was now.

We waited for word from Abelard that never came. I began to take on the duties of Marcel's personal servant, answering his call whenever he needed me. At night I brought him wine and brushed the mud from his boots. In the morning I served him bread and ale to break his fast; carried a bowl of water for him to wash his hands and face; fetched his hunting clothes, if he decided to ride out that day; and buckled his heavy leather belt around him, fastening the jeweled sheath that held his dagger. In the evenings, I sat through those interminable games of chess. It seemed I spent more time in his presence than did his wife, Lady Clarisse.

Then, two weeks before Christmas, a ripple of excitement went through the castle. A holy hermit, famed for working miracles, was reported to be on his way to Rambouillet.

"I don't want him inside here," Lady Clarisse announced. "I hear he's followed everywhere by a pack of filthy beggars, and he vows he will not enter any house unless he brings them with him."

"I can't turn him away, Clarisse," Marcel objected. "Especially in this holy season of Advent."

"Can't you build a shelter of some kind in the courtyard? They can have as much wood as they want for fires, and we'll feed them. I just don't want them in here."

Grudgingly, Marcel agreed. "I suppose we could give them straw to keep them off the cold ground and to cover themselves with. And there's the tent we put up for the last tournament—we could set that up in the courtyard."

Actually, I thought, the courtyard outside wouldn't be much colder than the inside of the castle, where the stone floors were frigid and the stone walls dripped with moisture. Heavy tapestries got hung on the walls to cut down on the chill. Rushes were spread underfoot to keep toes from going numb. Day and night, an open fire blazed in the middle of the great hall, although anyone standing farther than ten feet away from it still felt the cold.

Unlike ragged beggars, the inhabitants of the castle wore thick layers of clothing to protect themselves from the cold drafts entering through the window slits. Many of the ladies had long pockets sewn inside their sleeves where they kept little live animals—ermines or chipmunks or even rats—whose body heat warmed the ladies' arms. They were always crossing their arms in front of them, hugging themselves tightly under their bosoms to get the most heat from the small furry creatures that ran up and down inside their sleeves.

The warmest people in the castle were the cooks and serving girls who toiled in the kitchen house, where meals were prepared at all hours of the day and night. Girls were happy to serve as kitchen wenches, because they stayed close to the fires and always had enough to eat, stealing scraps from the great hall when the dishes were cleared away.

To roast an ox took twenty-four hours of turning a spit over a fire that had to be fed continuously, and that was what Marcel ordered now, that an ox be prepared for the holy hermit and his followers.

"You can't feed them an ox," Lady Clarisse objected. "It's Advent. Meat is forbidden."

Marcel answered, "The priest said they may be excused from their fast because they're traveling in harsh weather."

"You mean—we in the castle are to eat salt fish, while the beggars outside dine on roast ox? My lord, what are you thinking!"

Flushing, Marcel said, "It won't hurt us, my lady. Christmas will be here soon, and we'll all feast ourselves like gluttons for at least a week. Unless—shall we give the poor beggars fish now, and keep them here until Christmas, when everyone can eat roast ox? I mean, all of us, and the beggars, too?"

Lady Clarisse shuddered. "Feed them however you wish, my lord," she said, and escaped to the room where her ladies waited.

CHAPTER FIFTEEN

The day before the holy hermit and his followers reached us, the weather turned foul. A cold rain poured down on Marcel's men, who struggled to put up the tent, because the wetter the sailcloth got, the heavier it became. The courtyard turned into a sea of mud, churned by the boots of the half dozen workers who slogged through it, pounding stakes and tying ropes.

"They'll never get a fire going under here," one of the workmen grumbled.

"Not likely on this wet ground. You're right," another agreed.

"Then dig up some flagstones from around the well and carry them here," Lord Marcel ordered. "We'll build a makeshift hearth under the tent. Gather dry wood wherever you find it stacked, even if you have to take it from inside the peasants' huts."

What a contradiction Marcel was! Going to all this trouble to make things bearable for the hermit and his rabble, yet sending his men to pilfer wood from his own peasants, who would surely suffer when their winter kindling was gone.

He stood in the downpour, his long, dark hair hanging ropelike from beneath the bottom of his cap, his cape sodden, his boots soaked. This was a good-hearted man trying his best to provide alms for the poor. A man who'd taken me in and treated me more kindly than any servant had a right to expect. But he was blind to the misery of the people who toiled in his fields.

"And make sure you bring dry straw from inside the barns," he shouted after them. "Plenty of it— enough to soak up the damp from the ground, and more to go on top of that, so the beggars will sleep dry."

Standing beside Marcel, I was as soaked as he was. As we waited there dripping, a farmer from lands beyond Marcel's estate came galloping up on his horse. Water and mud splashed up in great arcs from the beast's hooves as the man shouted, "They're coming! The holy hermit and his people are about a mile down the road."

"Get that tent pole in place!" Marcel yelled. "Start the fire on those flagstones. Go to the kitchen and tell the cooks to bring the meat and the broth in wooden trenchers. Bread, too—don't forget the bread. And find as many torches as you can. We'll need them—it's getting dark."

Through the gathering gloom I saw the sad little procession drawing near to Rambouillet's gates. At the head of the ragged band, as tall and thin as the wooden staff he leaned on, came the hermit. He had on a torn gray robe tied around the middle with a frayed rope. It was similar to the Benedictine habit Abelard wore, but so dirty and bedraggled that if it was supposed to show what religious order the man belonged to, its identity had long since been lost. The hollows in his cheeks looked like craters. Rain dripped from his sparse gray beard. His feet were bare and muddy.

And yet—no matter how poor and thin and dirty the man appeared, as he came close to us, it was as if an aura of holiness reached out ahead of him and wrapped around each one of us. We all dropped to our knees in the mud.

"Rise! Rise!" the hermit called to us. "We are only poor travelers in Christ. We bring the peace of the Lord."

"Please, Brother," Marcel stammered, "take shelter under this tent—"

I knew Marcel well enough to see how embarrassed he was, wanting so badly to invite the paupers into the great hall, but having made a promise to his wife that he wouldn't. To hide his chagrin he shouted,

"Where is the food? Where are the torches? Spider, run inside and see why the food hasn't been brought out!"

Before I got halfway to the kitchen I met the servants coming toward me, bearing huge trays of meat and heavy pots of soup. A whole ox had been roasted, yet no more than twenty beggars arrived with the holy hermit. There was enough food to fill their bellies to bulging for a whole week. Or to last even longer, since the weather was cold enough to keep the meat from rotting before all the shreds got sucked away and the bones got gnawed through to the marrow.

They looked famished enough that I expected them to fall on the food like ravening wolves, but no, they waited for the hermit to offer a prayer of thanksgiving. It gave me time to study them, although even by torchlight, the gloom had become so thick it was hard to see. Most of them were wrapped in rags pulled over their heads to shelter them from the rain. As they pushed food into their hungry mouths, I saw that about half were men—mostly old men, gaunt and toothless, who needed to soften the bread in broth before they could eat it.

There were women and a few children who waited patiently while the old men ate. Then they crept forward to the soup pot, except for one small person—I couldn't tell whether it was male or female—who seemed to be cradling a child beneath a blanket that hid both of them from view.

The lords and ladies of the castle began to arrive then, crowding under the tent to get out of the rain.

"We're here! Has it begun yet?" Lady Clarisse asked loudly of her husband. "Have there been any miracles?"

Lord Marcel caught his lower lip between his teeth before he hissed, "This is not an entertainment, Clarisse. These people are not mimes or jongleurs or minstrels."

Lady Clarisse flushed at the rebuke in his voice. "You said the hermit worked miracles," she murmured.

"But not on demand!" Turning on his heel, he said, "Eat heartily, everyone." And then to me, "Spider, that beggar under the blanket over there— he hasn't eaten. Take something to him."

I filled a wooden bowl with soup before I picked my way across the mud, treading carefully between the people who huddled next to the fire. Their hunched shadows, cast upon the yellow-and-red-striped sailcloth, looked ludicrous against the tent's vivid colors. Steam rose from the rags of the paupers huddled closest to the fire; steam billowed from the chilled breaths of those too far from the hearth to feel its warmth. Marcel's peasants, who'd been allowed to come, held torches aloft; the orange flames sputtered and wavered, creating additional grotesque shadows that stretched to the peak of the tent, where flags had flown during the tournament the summer before.

I tugged on the blanket of the person I'd been told to bring food to. As the blanket fell open slightly, I saw the pinched face of a small child whose enormous eyes looked out at me. Gently, I pulled the rest of the blanket away. My heart leaped with recognition.

Flore!

Whether from exhaustion or weakness, her arms had grown slack around the little girl. Placing my own arm behind Flore's back, I raised her and held the bowl next to her lips.

"Bless you, sir," she whispered. "But feed the child."

And as she stared right at me, I realized she didn't know me. Perhaps it was because so much time had passed, or because the firelight behind my back meant my face was in shadow, or because my nice clothes made me look like a high-ranking servant— whatever the reason, she didn't remember who I was.

She looked ghastly! So weak, she seemed close to death. The baby appeared to be healthier, probably because Flore had given most of her own food to the child for who knows how long. I stayed with her until both she and the tiny girl had drunk from the bowl.

Meanwhile, the lords and ladies shuffled their feet with impatience, waiting for something to happen. They hadn't come outside on such a stormy night just to witness beggars eating.

"Let's have a miracle or two," one of the lords called out. He and his lady had ridden from their own estate the day before, envious because Rambouillet was to receive a visit from this holy man of great reputation, while other nearby estates were not.

Worried, I settled Flore with the blanket around her and went to find Lord Marcel. Somehow I had to convince him that Flore needed shelter, that she had to be taken inside, out of the bad weather, in spite of what Lady Clarisse had decreed. Flore looked so wasted, I was afraid she might die on the spot. I tugged Marcel's sleeve to get his attention.

"What is it, Spider?" he asked. As he looked down at me, his eyes began to widen. "Of course! Why didn't I think of it? I know what you want—" Half lifting me, he dragged me across the mud and stopped in front of the holy man. "Brother, here's a boy who needs a miracle," he announced. "He's been mute since birth. Can you make him talk?"

"All things are possible in Christ," the hermit replied.

Aghast at what was happening, I struggled in Marcel's arms, but then something burst in my mind and I stopped fighting and hung limp. Why not? I thought. That would make it easier to get help for Flore.

As thin as he was, the hermit had great strength in his hands. He clamped them around my throat until I thought I would choke. When I gasped for air, he shouted—and his voice was as strong as his fingers— "'And they brought to Jesus one deaf and dumb . . .'"

"No, he's not deaf—," I heard Marcel say through the fog that was clouding over me because I could hardly breathe.

"'. . . and they entreated Jesus to lay his hand upon him. And spitting, Jesus touched the man's tongue.'"

His hands tightened around my throat until I gagged and my tongue stuck out. He spat on it.

"'And looking up to heaven, Jesus sighed and said to him, "Ephpheta," that is, "Be thou opened." And the bond of the man's tongue was loosed, and he began to speak correctly.'"

Abruptly, the hermit let go of me. Released that suddenly, I fell and landed with my head near the fire. Everyone had become so deathly silent that I heard the burning sticks hiss as their sap bubbled. "Is he dead?" someone whispered.

No, I wasn't dead, but I had to fight for each breath. Smells overpowered me: wood smoke, the pungent reek of pitch burning in torches, the stench of scorched meat, wet wool, and unwashed bodies. I gagged until Marcel dragged me to my feet and pounded my back.

Phlegm rattled in my throat while I struggled to take in air; moments passed until at last my thoughts began to clear. When I could breathe again, I filled my lungs with as much breath as they could hold and shouted out, "Praise Jesus!"

Pandemonium erupted. Marcel wept. Lady

Clarisse looked triumphant—she had her tour de force now, a marvel that would be talked about for years throughout the entire countryside. The peasants—because they all knew me—yelled, "Spider can talk! He has a voice! The holy man cured him!" They surged around and lifted me high into the air, like a trophy of war. Others pressed forward in a crush, reaching out to touch the hermit, hoping that a bit of the miraculous would rub off on them, too.

"Miracle! Miracle! Miracle!" they shouted. Lord Marcel tried to reach up and embrace me, but I was held so high, he could only take my hand and cry, "God has touched you, Spider. No wonder Abelard singled you out! He could tell there was something about you—"

"We will reward the boy," Lady Clarisse announced to one and all, as though I'd just unseated a foe in a tournament like the one they'd hosted last summer. "Name anything you wish for, Spider."

It had been so long since I'd spoken—at least prior to that first "Praise Jesus!"—that I had to keep coughing and clearing my throat to frame the next words. Someone cried, "Give him wine," and a goblet was thrust into my hands. I tried to take a sip, but I was being jostled so much by the men still holding me up high that the wine spilled all over me.

"Put him down!" Marcel thundered, and they did, but the crowd stayed so noisy that Marcel had to bend down to hear what I said.

"A woman over there—," I began, and had to cough again. "A child is with her. They're weak—bring them to my bed. That's all the reward I want."

At that, Lady Clarisse took a step backward, but she couldn't break her promise, not in front of her friends. All of them had heard her tell me, "Name anything you wish for." And I had just done that.

Which is how, in a teeming rainstorm, it came about that Lord Marcel carried Flore into his castle. I followed with the little girl in my arms. I could tell Marcel was eager to get back to the tent to see whether any other miracles had happened during his absence. Rather carelessly, he dropped Flore onto my bed and said, "You can tell me tomorrow—since you can speak now, praise God—why you've taken an interest in this ugly, deformed woman. If you're thinking about trying to bring her back to health—well, to my eye, Spider, she looks too far gone. The baby might be saved, though. Call for anything you need: food or blankets or extra candles—" And he was gone.

Flore seemed to have fallen unconscious, but the little girl watched me, her eyes unafraid, as I went into the hall and cried out for one of the servants to bring a sheepskin. I surprised myself when I heard how loud I could shout. After the maidservant came running in answer to my call, she looked all around to see who had summoned her.

"I called you," I told her impatiently, and at the

sound of my still-raspy voice she threw her hands over her ears as if she'd heard a ghost. "It's all right, I'm able to talk now. The hermit worked a miracle on me," I told her, lying out loud for the first time. In the tent, I'd let people deceive *themselves* about the supposed miracle. Now, with the words I spoke to that woman, I'd begun to build my own web of lies. And I would go on weaving it, strand upon strand, for as long as I needed to.

With shaking hands the maidservant followed my orders to remove Flore's wet, ragged clothing. When she got a look at Flore's twisted spine and humped back, she turned ashen and made the sign of the cross. Between my sudden ability to talk and Flore's amazing ugliness, the poor servant must have thought a devil had been set loose in the room. She stammered, "Is—is she the child's—?"

"The child's mother," I finished for her, and I saw the doubt that filled the woman's eyes.

"How can—? She's too old and hideous!" she exclaimed. "And the child is lovely!"

"Cover both of them with the sheepskin and try to find dry clothing for them," I told her. The more I talked, the easier it was becoming, although I noted with disappointment that my voice still sounded high. A whole year had passed since I'd last heard myself speak, and in all that time the timbre hadn't deepened one bit.

Pointing to Flore, the servant said, "She'll need a dress small enough to fit a ten-year-old."

"It doesn't matter about the fit," I told her. "Just find something that will keep them warm. Bring candles, and milk for the child—sweetened with honey." I knew nothing about what a small child could eat, but milk and honey shouldn't hurt her.

The servant was glad to get away. In a little while she returned with the things I'd asked for. "Dress the two of them," I told her, "and then you can go."

Whether Flore was still unconscious or had just fallen into a deep sleep of exhaustion, I couldn't tell, but she didn't move as the serving maid pulled a warm wool dress over her. After the woman tucked the sheepskin around mother and child, she turned to go, but hesitated. "Why didn't they ask for a miracle for *her?*" she wondered, gesturing toward Flore. "Instead of you."

I just shook my head. How could I tell her that the whole miracle had been a fake? A pretense—at least on my part. Probably the holy hermit believed he'd actually cured me. Maybe he'd worked real miracles before. At least people said that he had. But what happened out there under the tent proved how easily people could be fooled: They'd come to see a spectacle, they'd believed they were going to see a spectacle, and I'd connived to give them one.

The whole time I'd lived at Rambouillet I'd never spoken a word out loud, so it was natural for people to think I *couldn't* talk. I'd been content to let them think it. Then, after the holy man had nearly strangled me and had spit on my tongue, I'd shouted out, like an actor on a stage, "Praise—!" Remembering it, I hung my head in shame.

After the servant left, I sat in the silent alcove, condemning myself as the candles burned down through the long hours of the night, dripping wax like tears on the cold stone floor. More than a year earlier I'd made two vows: One, that the first person to hear my voice would be Abelard; and two, that I never would use words to deceive. I'd broken both those vows in one brief act. The first didn't matter that much, but the second did. The lies, the fakery, the sham—they were going to haunt me for as long as I remained at Rambouillet.

I had the urge to leave right then, to go find Abelard, wherever he was. But I couldn't abandon Flore, who lay so ill on my bed, breathing shallowly and moaning in her sleep. I was responsible for her now, and I almost hated her for it. It was because of Flore that I'd trapped myself in this web.

The sheepskin moved, and the child wiggled out from under it. She slid down the side of the bed and landed with her feet on the frigid floor. I had no idea how old she was, but she seemed able to walk well enough. Almost on tiptoe she came over to me and put her tiny hand in mine.

Looking up at me with those huge brown eyes, she asked, "What's your name?"

So she was old enough to talk! "Aran," I answered. "What's yours?"

"Joie." Then she held up three fingers.

"Are you three?" I asked, and she nodded. She was so small, it was hard to believe she was all of three years old, but Rabel had said she'd been tiny at birth, and certainly she looked underfed now.

I'd forgotten about the bowl of milk the servant had left. "Would you like this, Joie?" I asked, offering it to her. "Drink it and then get back under the covers."

She held the bowl to her mouth and drained it, the whole time staring at me over the rim with those enormous, hunger-shadowed eyes. When she finished, she said, "Thank you, Aran."

It was the first time since my mother's death that I'd heard my name spoken softly and sweetly, without a loud curse added to it by my father or brother. A heavy weight lifted from my chest. Smiling, I carried Joie to the bed and settled her next to her mother.

CHAPTER SIXTEEN

AT DAYLIGHT, BEFORE I TOOK BREAD TO LORD Marcel, I held the bright steel blade of his dagger next to Flore's mouth. Joie watched me, her dark eyes grave but unafraid. How could she trust me so completely—this stranger who was standing over her mother with a knife? To reassure her, I gave a slight nod.

A small circle of moisture fogged the blade. That meant Flore was still breathing, although she'd felt so cold to my touch, I was afraid she'd died during the night. Sliding the dagger into its sheath, I bent over her and whispered, "Flore, do you hear me?"

"She can't," Joie answered. "Mama's sleeping."

"You're right. I want you to stay here beside your mama, Joie," I told her. "Will you do that? When I come back, I'll bring you something nice to eat."

"First I have to go to the bushes," she said.

"To the bushes?" After a moment I understood what she meant, but I had no wish to explain to a three-year-old that in a castle in the middle of winter, buckets were used for bodily relief and got emptied into the fields every day. I started to point to the bucket in my corner, but thought better of it and summoned a serving girl.

After helping Lord Marcel into his linen surcoat, I mumbled some lame excuse to him that since God had given me a miracle, I wanted to do good for others in need, starting with Flore, which is why I had to hurry back to her right away. When I returned to my alcove I found not one but three serving women there, fussing over Joie. One was feeding her boiled oats and cream from a spoon, another twined Joie's dark hair around her fingers to make ringlets, while the third rubbed Joie's feet to warm them. Totally absorbed in the child, the three women ignored Flore, who lay unmoving: a small, still mound beneath the sheepskin.

"Look at her little toes! They're blue! We must find her stockings and shoes to wear." The servants frowned at me as if it were my fault Joie's toes felt cold.

"Fine," I answered. "Take her with you and do whatever you can for her, but get off the bed so I can help the mother."

All three of them began to laugh. "It's true," they giggled to one another. "Spider can talk now! He sounds strange, but he really is speaking. Say something else, Spider."

"Go away! No—wait! First fetch some broth. And have someone heat rocks in the hearth, and when they're hot enough, wrap them in rags and bring them here to warm the bed for this sick woman."

"Oooh, listen!" one of the serving girls cried. "The words come pouring out of him, but his voice sounds as shrill as a shepherd's flute."

"Like a girl's," another said.

"That's because he's still very young, aren't you, Spider?" the third murmured. "Tell us how old you are, Spider."

"Never mind! Just go!" I shouted, then repeated it more softly, with a "please," since I didn't want to frighten Joie.

As soon as they'd gone I turned my attention to Flore. Although her eyes were closed, she'd begun to writhe and moan, rubbing her stick-thin arms across the sheepskin. Her fingers groped, searching for her child.

"Joie is safe," I assured her. "She's been fed and she'll be cared for. Flore, do you hear me now? Can you look at me?"

As though her eyelids were weighted down with heavy stones, she struggled to open them. When at last she peered at me through fogged eyes, I could tell that she still didn't know me.

"I'm Aran," I told her. "Years ago, my brother brought me to Master Galien's house. They welded a metal shell around me to turn me into a spider like Rabel. You cared for me—"

"The pretty one!" she gasped. "Abelard took you away."

I sank to my knees beside the bed. "Yes, that's who I was. Who I am. I couldn't talk then, but I can talk now because last night the hermit worked a miracle—"

Why was I telling that lie to this poor, sick woman who might not even live? "My name is Aran," I said again, taking hold of her small, clawlike hand, which felt as cold as death. "I'm going to make you well."

"Joie . . . ," she murmured.

"Joie has already found her way into the hearts of the servants. They're taking good care of her, and they'll bring her back here soon." Just then two men arrived with heated rocks wrapped in rags. We placed them close to Flore's emaciated body. When the broth was brought, I spooned a bit of it into her slack lips, but she had so much trouble swallowing that I was afraid it would choke her.

The next week was like a bad dream. I hardly slept. I couldn't neglect my duties as Lord Marcel's personal servant—if his boots weren't kept clean and the hem of his cloak brushed free of mud, Lady Clarisse might complain; if she did, Lord Marcel, who always tried to keep peace with his wife, might put Flore and Joie out into the cold. Thank God it was nearly Christmas and the castle was full of guests: That meant I didn't need to play those endless games of chess in the evenings.

Since the servants grumbled about having to heat the rocks that warmed Flore where she lay, I took over that job myself. At night I slept across the foot of the bed so that if Flore should call out, I would hear her.

Each free moment I had, I coaxed Flore to eat. She seemed to do best with small bits of bread broken into warm milk. On good days, she might swallow a spoonful or two, and then Joie would finish off what was left. The hungry look had begun to disappear from Joie's eyes. Yet poor Flore only became more emaciated.

As I knelt beside the bed begging Flore to take just one more sip, I thought about the strange circle of events that had brought us around to this. How I must have pained Flore, those few years ago, when I'd refused to eat! Because of stubbornness, I *wouldn't* eat for her, no matter how much she coaxed. Because of weakness, now, Flore *couldn't* eat for me, no matter how hard I begged. Desperate to get food into her, I realized how much anguish I must have caused her back then. Silently, I asked her to forgive me.

At last, on the Feast of the Epiphany, Flore managed to eat a whole bowl of soup. I felt triumphant. By February, she could sit halfway up in bed.

"So your beggar woman is going to live after all,"

Lord Marcel said. "Rabel tells Lady Clarisse that the woman has become strong enough to leave here."

"Oh, no," I cried. "She can't walk. She can barely stand."

"Lady Clarisse says—," Marcel began. "Or rather, both of us agree—that we are willing to have Flore taken by cart to an almshouse where she'll be fed by monks whose job it is to care for the poor. The child, too."

Huddled in a cold almshouse with paupers who were fed barely enough to stay alive—Flore would be dead in a week! Then what would happen to Joie?

"Lord Marcel," I began, "did Rabel happen to tell Lady Clarisse how we know Flore? That she was the cook in Master Galien's house where both Rabel and I were kept? That Flore is probably the finest cook in France?"

"Really? As sickly as she is, though, she could never work in a kitchen again."

"I'm not so sure. If we keep her at Rambouillet, she wouldn't have to work as hard," I argued. "She could sit in a chair and supervise. Flore knows secrets about cooking that even the king's chefs would kill to steal. If she stays here, you can serve the finest food to be found on any estate for miles around. Better than Paris, even. That would please Lady Clarisse, wouldn't it?"

I was making it up as I went along, lying again, but I didn't care. "Ask Rabel. He'll tell you. It was Flore's wonderful food that made Rabel's arms and legs grow so long during all those years he lived at Master Galien's. If it hadn't been for Flore, your famous Rabel would look much more ordinary. In fact, your father-in-law probably wouldn't have bought him at all, and then the ladies wouldn't be entertained by all his songs they like so much and your guests wouldn't tell everyone that you and Lady Clarisse own the most interesting human oddity in the whole countryside—"

Lord Marcel looked at me strangely, and no wonder—I was babbling. "Calm yourself, Spider," he said. "If it means so much to you, we'll put Flore in the kitchen house for a month and see how she does."

As soon as I could get away, I ran to find Rabel. As usual, he was lounging at the feet of the ladies, plucking the strings of his lute, inventing worthless songs to amuse them. They obviously valued him: I noticed that someone had decorated the neck of his tunic with a row of gold stitches.

I entered the big room and stood unmoving in the middle of it. Surprised, the ladies stopped their embroidering to stare at me.

"It's Spider," Lady Clarisse exclaimed. "My lord Marcel's servant. The boy who was cured by a miracle. Now that he can talk, perhaps he'll tell us all about Abelard and Eloise. He was servant to them, too, you know, before he came here."

Scowling, Rabel scrambled awkwardly to his feet and took a few steps toward me.

"B-beg pardon, Lady Clarisse," I stammered. "I'm s-still—not used—to t-talking." One more lie. I gestured to Rabel that I wanted him to follow me out of the room.

In the hall, I dragged him into a shadowed recess in the wall. "Listen," I hissed, "you have to do something for me because if you don't, I'm going to tell those ladies every story I can think of about Abelard and Eloise, and they'll give me all the attention you get now and you'll be kicked out of the way like last year's rotten straw."

Furious, Rabel grabbed me by the shoulders. He tried to fling me against the stone wall, but his long arms had very little strength in them. Although I wasn't very muscular myself, I easily overpowered him. With my elbow pressed hard against his neck, I muttered, "Do you want me to go back in there to Lady Clarisse, or are you ready to make a bargain?"

He couldn't answer because I was pushing hard against his windpipe. If the look in his eyes had been a knife, I'd have been dead.

"Bargain?" I asked again.

Rabel nodded.

"All right." I turned him loose. "Those ladies believe the things you say to them. I want you to tell them that Flore is the greatest cook in France."

"Flore?" Rabel rubbed his neck. "That's probably true."

"Lord Marcel's going to let her work in the

kitchen house for a month, supervising the cooks. In that month, you keep praising the food to the ladies — they're so easily led by you that they'll start praising it, too. Make up a song about it if you need to."

"So . . . ," Rabel sneered, "I gather that you want Flore to stay. What do you get out of all of this if she does? That ugly old hag in your bed every night? Or is it the beautiful little girl you're after?"

I hit him hard, but I only managed to bruise my knuckles against the iron shell he still wore. Rabel laughed uproariously, then leaned forward until his pale, unearthly eyes were only two inches from mine. "I'll do what you want, miracle boy, but only if you stay out of my territory. Forever! If you come weasling your way around my ladies, Flore will be out of here so fast, you'll be speechless — again!"

With mutual hatred, we glared at one another, but the bargain had been sealed.

Some of the field-workers, who were idle during the winter months, anyway, helped me weave a chair out of willow wands. We shaped it so that Flore could lean back in it. That way she'd be able to breathe easier. When she tried to stand or sit straight up, pressure from her spine — which was a lot more curved now than when I'd first known her — pinched her lungs.

Flore was too smart to start immediately bossing the kitchen wenches. For the first few days she contented herself with learning where everything was kept. Joie ran back and forth, bringing whatever her mother asked for—herbs, spoons, sieves, live quail in a cage—which Flore inspected while she made mental lists of what she would need. She sniffed the butter and wrinkled her nose if it was rancid; fingered the flour to feel whether it had been ground fine enough; tasted the honey, because honey varied according to the kind of flowers the bees sucked.

Little by little, Flore began to make suggestions. "Try a bit of tarragon in the soup, why don't you." Or, "If you score the ham this way"—and she would demonstrate with a sharp knife—"those Arabian cloves will go deeper inside and their taste will spread farther." And, "Such lovely mushrooms! Let's chop them, mix them with minced walnuts, and stuff the roast woodhen with them. Only, add more butter."

I never knew whether Rabel kept his part of the bargain. It might not have been necessary, since Flore's meals were so sumptuous that everyone—the men as well as the ladies—commented on the improvement.

The kitchen house was the perfect place for Flore to be, because it was always warm. And with all the tasting she needed to do, she finally ate enough to stay alive. As long as she kept reclining she had little trouble breathing—a trapdoor hole in the ceiling let most of the irritating smoke escape. When a fire blazed high on the hearth, the smoke hole could be opened by a long pole fastened on one end to the trapdoor. The other end fitted into a wall bracket.

Many's the time I worked it myself, lifting the pole—which rested on the floor when it wasn't in use—and sliding the end into the bracket, thus propping open a vent. Freed that way, the hearth smoke always drifted upward and out.

I began to think about the smoke-filled huts where the peasants lived. When they had no dry wood and were forced to scour the damp forests for anything that would burn, the thick smoke from their cooking fires had nowhere to escape to. It would hang heavily inside their small hovels, choking the people who lived, ate, and slept there. All winter long they coughed, especially the children. During the past winter alone, nine children on the estate had died from coughing sickness.

Why couldn't the peasants have smoke holes in the ceilings of their huts, I wondered. I thought about what I'd told Marcel (even though it was a lie): that because God had given me a miracle, I wanted to do good for other people in need. If I actually tried to do good, would that make the lie less sinful?

"Lord Marcel," I blurted the next morning after I'd fastened his short cape across his shoulders, "I'd like to help the peasants by putting smoke holes in the ceilings of their huts."

"They'd never use them," Lord Marcel answered, spearing a bit of cheese with the tip of his dagger.

"Would you let me try?" I asked. "It's about—my wish to help others."

"Ah, yes. Well, Spider, you did receive a miracle from God through his holy hermit; there's no doubt about that since I saw it with my own eyes. And that crippled woman Flore has worked out well enough." He spit out a bit of cheese rind and murmured, "Hmmm, perhaps God actually does want to reach my peasants through you. Otherwise I'd never consider what you just said about smoke holes because I think it's utter foolishness. I'd swear it will never work, unless you can call up another miracle. But, who knows—maybe you can. Suppose we start with only three of the huts and see what happens."

Spring had come by then. The days were sunny and warm, and Flore begged me to take Joie along. "If you'll be outside, anyway, working on those thatched roofs, you can let her run in the sunshine. Her cheeks are nice and round these days, but she's pale as flour."

Lord Marcel allowed me to choose the three huts that were to have smoke holes. There was a lot of grumbling because the peasants agreed with Lord Marcel that it was a foolish idea, but they were afraid to oppose me too fiercely, because I was, as Rabel had called me, the miracle boy. The one God's finger had touched.

I chose the huts with the sickliest children inside, children who were still coughing even though winter had ended. The work was easy enough—the men climbed the ladder with me, and we began by pulling up a patch of thatch on each roof. Then we'd cut a square through the sticks that made up the roof, lash the sticks together to form a sturdy small door, and fasten a pole from the inside to raise and lower it. It worked the same as the much larger trapdoor in the castle's kitchen house.

The weather stayed warm. Joie's cheeks turned pink. The women who lived in the three huts exclaimed with pleasure that their smoke did, indeed, rise up through the vents in the roof, and their babies didn't cough as much. Everyone who saw me — shepherds or field-workers, dairymaids or geese girls, the blacksmith, the stonecutter, the horse trainer, the stable lads — all smiled and called out, "There's Spider. He can talk now. God gave him a miracle so he could help us."

And I felt less guilty. Was it so bad to let a falsehood go on existing if it made things better? I tried to think of other ways I might improve the lives of the peasants, and came up with one more possibility.

For rent on the land, Lord Marcel took a portion of the peasants' hay, hides, grain, butter — if they had any — and wool.

"Lord Marcel," I began, more boldly now because my first project had been a success, "I've been considering. Every family on the estate keeps a certain allotment of wool after each year's shearing. The women spin it to make yarn to weave their clothes, but they're not very good at spinning."

"And so?"

"I could teach them to spin better. My mother spun the finest yarn in all the countryside around Rouen, and she taught me."

"Then the peasants would wear clothes that looked a little nicer. Do you really believe that would make much difference in their lives, Spider?"

"Wait, my lord, you haven't heard the rest. The women and girls who learn to spin best—and some are bound to be more skillful than others—will give me their yarn. I'll sell it in Paris. I know where there's a cloth-maker who pays a fair price. My brother took me there the first time I ever saw Paris."

"And so you'll get money from the cloth-maker," Marcel went on, "but the women who gave you their yarn won't have any of it left to make into winter clothes for their children."

"They'll share!" I cried. "The ones whose yarn isn't as fine will share it with the others, because it doesn't have to be perfect if it's used for peasant tunics. And when I bring back the money from the sale of the really good yarn, all the workers on the estate will share that, too. Then they can buy themselves things like needles and nails, and hatchets to cut more kindling so they won't be so cold in the winter—"

"Oh, Spider." Lord Marcel sighed. "You don't know much about how peasants think."

Of course I did. Hadn't I been a poor shepherd boy? I knew my plan would work. "Let me try," I begged. "The sheep will be sheared in two weeks. I'll help with the shearing, and then I'll help with the spinning, and I'll teach the women to spin the way my mother taught me."

Lord Marcel shook his head. "If it weren't that God has singled you out by letting the hermit cure you, I'd never go along with such an impossible scheme. But I'm willing to let you do it—once—just to see if God really is working through you in some mysterious way. I need to know because . . ." He paused. "I want an heir, and Lady Clarisse hasn't . . ." Lowering his eyes, he said, "If I strike a bargain with God by letting you do what you suggest, perhaps . . ." Lord Marcel didn't seem able to finish his sentences. He took the dagger out of his belt and held it reverently before his eyes, because the dagger was, of course, shaped exactly like a pointed cross. "God's mysterious ways," he murmured again.

At the end of the summer, long past the shearing, after the wool had been spun, but before I'd had a chance to take it to Paris, everything changed. A message arrived from Abelard.

He wanted me to come immediately.

CHAPTER SEVENTEEN

ABELARD'S SUCCESS AT THE PARACLETE, where ever-growing crowds of students had joined him in the wilderness to hear him preach and teach, had infuriated his enemies. In a scheme to banish him even farther away, they elevated him to the priesthood and made him abbot at Saint-Gildas de Rhuys, on the coast of Brittany. That was where Father Abbot Peter Abelard now wanted me to come.

I was glad to be going back to Brittany in the summertime. I remembered the happy days there with Denise and Hugh, before Astrolabe was born. But Joie sobbed, "Please don't go, Aran. I don't want you to go."

"You won't even know I'm not here," I teased her. "The way everyone fusses over you—a royal princess couldn't have more admirers than you have, Joie. They give you the sweetest berries to eat, and the liveliest puppies and kittens to play with, and that pretty white dove in a cage. And—what's that in your hair? Another new ribbon? Again?"

"Stay here!" she wailed.

"I'll come back one day," I told her. "Maybe sooner than any of us thinks. You just keep taking good care of your mama. Promise me that."

Lord Marcel also seemed a bit reluctant to have me leave. "I'm giving you a horse," he said, "so you can make your journey more quickly. He's yours to keep. His name is Charlemagne." Stroking the horse's mane, Marcel added, "He's a gelding, so he's easy to manage."

I wondered about that. Since that night when Fulbert had attacked him, Abelard had become a gelding, too, and he was anything but manageable. Wherever he went he caused trouble.

Still, the horse Lord Marcel gave me was a fine one—not large, but then I didn't need a big war horse since I wasn't riding into battle. Charlemagne was a sorrel, tightly muscled and tireless. Seated on Charlemagne, with saddlebags packed full of provisions, and wearing colorful and well-made clothes, I easily could have passed for a boy from the upper classes. A landowner's son, highborn.

Which is exactly what they took me for. I couldn't bear it when on the road, beggars ran after me holding out their hands, or lifting up their half-starved children: At the end of the first day I'd given away all the food in Charlemagne's saddlebags.

Even though I had money, I couldn't find a monastery where I could spend the night, and I was afraid to sleep in the forest. Wearing fine clothes and riding a well-bred horse would make me a sure target for robbers, who might beat me or murder me. So I kept riding all night long that first night. Poor Charlemagne. No wonder rich people paid men-at-arms to protect them when they traveled.

Once again I was heading toward Brittany, the land where Abelard had been born. I couldn't help contrasting this trip with the earlier one, when Abelard and Eloise and I had felt so much promise as we'd traveled the road together. That had been during a joyous spring; now it was sweaty summer. Yet when I reached the forest of Brocéliande this time, it felt just as magical as before. I wondered if Merlin, that old wizard, was still there in his layers of air, highly amused by the web I'd been caught in.

The monastery of Saint-Gildas, to which I was journeying, had been built on the stormy seacoast of Brittany. It was almost in the shadow of the ancient menhirs and the tomb of that pagan chieftain, where I'd wished so hard for my tongue to be loosened. What a malevolent turn of events had made my wish come true! That old pagan must be laughing in his tomb, I thought. Everything that had happened to Abelard and Eloise and me was so astonishingly different from the dreams we'd spun on our first journey through Brocéliande. Sorcerers or seers or God the

Father and Son and Holy Ghost: Just one breath from them was all it took, and the delicate strands of a web like mine would hang in shreds.

I had a chance to get a first long look at the Abbey of Saint-Gildas from the clifftop above before riding down to its gate. Below me, the storm-whipped sea pounded against the gray, barren seawall. The abbey was a harsh, low-flung place, all on one level, with no beauty around it—no trees, flowers, or wind-swept bushes, nothing but rock. It looked more like a fortress than a house of prayer.

Tired, disheveled, and hungry after my nine-day ride, I arrived at the abbey during the supper hour. No one even noticed me, and if they'd noticed, I doubt they'd have cared much. The monks sprawled across tables, grabbing food, spilling wine, eating like barbarians, and throwing scraps to a pack of dogs who leaped onto the table for more. They spoke in some rough kind of local dialect that sounded completely different from the Breton tongue that Denise and Hugh and Ralph Abelard spoke.

The dogs weren't the worst of it. If there was a celibate monk in all of Saint-Gildas, he didn't seem to be in the dining hall that evening. These men had their concubines right there in the monastery with them, pulling them onto their laps, fondling them right out in the open. Some even had their children beside them.

Suddenly, Abelard burst into the room. He strode

to a table, knocked plates and bones and dogs off its surface, and climbed up on top of it.

In that voice of his that could fill a whole cathedral, he roared, "Clear this room! How many times have I told you to get rid of the women and children and animals? Do it now! For your penance, you will come to the refectory at compline and stay on your knees until matins."

If only he'd stopped there, they might have obeyed him, because his voice was still powerful and his manner commanding. But staring down on them, he curled his lip and spat out, "You men are *pigs!*"

Of course they resented him. Even though they behaved like pigs, they didn't like to be called that. I could see the defiance in their eyes as Abelard stormed out of the dining room. I hurried to follow him, because I was afraid to be caught in the midst of those brutish Norman monks. What would they do to me if they noticed me there—a stranger in their hall? I didn't wait to find out.

I caught up to Abelard barely in time: He was about to slam shut the door of his room and bar it from inside, as I learned he always did, for his own protection.

"Spider!" he cried. "Welcome to hell. How did you get here?"

"I came on horseback," I told him, waiting for him to exclaim over my being able to speak.

But he didn't. Instead, he said, "For God's sake,

where did you leave the horse? Hurry and get it before my monks find it. If they reach it before you do, the horse will be stolen and sold, or maybe butchered and eaten."

"What am I supposed to do with it?" I asked, still waiting for him to say something about my talking.

"Bring it inside and put it in the room right next to mine. It has a bar on the door, too."

"Inside? Here?" I couldn't believe it.

"Just hurry! And when you get the horse into the room, you stay there with it and bar the door from the inside."

It felt so unreal, it was like a wild dream. I had to tug hard on Charlemagne's bridle, because even though my horse was easy to handle, he didn't much like being brought into a dwelling, and he barely fit through the door of the room. It was a small room, just a cell with nothing in it, not even a mound of straw to sit on. That was just as well, because Charlemagne might have tried to eat it, since it seemed neither of us was going to be fed that night. Except through a very small hole at the top of the outside wall, no light entered the room, and the evening was fading fast.

A panel slid open in the inside wall. Abelard's face appeared, illuminated by a candle. "I just realized," he said. "You're talking. How did that come about?"

So he'd finally noticed! "Do you remember," I

began, "on the night that Fulbert hurt you—?"

"I recall hardly anything about that night," he interrupted. "Only that I'd been sleeping soundly and then Fulbert and his man came at me with a knife. And soon the room was filled with my students, who carried me to a doctor."

So he had no memory of cutting my tongue! Before I could tell him about it, he grunted, "We don't have time to talk. You must get out of here before my monks try to kill you the way they're always trying to kill me."

He seemed suspicious to the point of wild exaggeration. Or had he gone a little mad? Maybe the loss of his manhood weighed on him so heavily that he imagined everyone was trying to harm him. Even though he said there was no time for us to talk, that didn't stop him from pouring out all his own fears and troubles to me as we stood there in the near darkness, one on each side of a wall, looking at each other through the small opening.

The monks stole from him, he said. They set traps to trip him on the stone stairs outside the building— hoping, I suppose, that he'd fall and break his neck. They kept trying to poison him, which was why he never ate any of the food they fixed.

If even half of what Abelard told me was true, this was the roughest bunch of supposedly religious men I'd ever heard of. No wonder the monks of Saint-Denis had sent Abelard here! They wanted him destroyed, and Saint-Gildas was the hellhole that would do it.

"Look into my room," he told me, moving away from the little window so I could see past him. A few candles burned on a table where at least twenty manuscript pages lay unbound. "See these?" As I watched, he picked up the pages, started to roll them together, and said, "Spider, I sent for you because I want you to be my messenger. Take this letter to Marcel DuChesne. He'll understand what he must do with it." He paused, then, peering at me closely, he asked, "How is Marcel? Is he well?"

"Well. But unhappy."

"Why?"

"He wants an heir, and Lady Clarisse hasn't given him one."

Abelard shrugged, as though Marcel's lack of an heir wasn't of any real importance. "I'll write him a few lines," he said, and quickly cut a new point on a quill before dipping it into a horn of ink.

While I waited, I tried to soothe Charlemagne, who didn't much like where he was. His neck quivered under my touch. "You're hungry, I know," I whispered. "I am, too."

When Abelard finally passed the manuscript through the opening to me, he said, "You're the only person I can trust to deliver this. You're always inconspicuous. No one would ever suspect you of carrying anything worth stealing."

So much for my theory that I looked like a rich man's son! Abelard's words made me realize how little he knew about me now. At Rambouillet, I was anything but inconspicuous. Everyone there recognized me—I was their miracle boy. Abelard hadn't given me a chance to tell him about the changes in my life; to him, I was still Spider, the humble, silent servant who obeyed his every wish.

I wanted at least to tell him that my name was Aran, but before I could speak he said, "I ordered the monks to go to the refectory for compline, the hour for evening prayers. But who knows whether they'll obey me? They seldom do. Still, that hour will be your best chance to escape, Spider."

His expression softened, and for the first time I caught a glimpse of the old Abelard. Reaching through the opening in the wall, he took my hand and said, "I can't stress to you strongly enough, Spider, how important this letter is to me. It *must* reach Marcel. Especially if the monks here actually succeed in killing me."

His grip tightened on my hand. "After Marcel reads the letter, he'll have it copied. But I want you to read it, too, Spider. You can read, I remember. That summer, when we were all together, I taught you from the books I'd had as a schoolboy—"

His eyes filled with tears, but he brushed them away and announced abruptly, "I'm leaving now for the refectory. Here, I'll give you a candle so you won't have to wait in the dark. When the candle burns down half an inch, unbar the door, lead your horse outside, and ride like the wind away from this loathsome pit. We'll meet again—God willing—in a less tormented time and place."

CHAPTER EIGHTEEN

ALL THE WAY BACK TO RAMBOUILLET I worried about Abelard. Had he gone strange in the head? To have me bring a horse inside a monastery—was that the act of a rational man?

Certainly he'd behaved erratically, but when I pictured those monks of Saint-Gildas, I felt chills along my spine. It was easy enough to believe they were thieves and murderers. Even though I'd been inside the dining hall for only a few minutes, I could tell how much they hated Abelard.

Abelard had never been cowardly; if he was afraid now, he must have a good reason to be. I couldn't wait for the chance to read the letter he'd written Lord Marcel.

When I reached Rambouillet I went straight to the room where I usually found Marcel. I pulled out the thick scroll of pages and handed it to him. "For you," I said. "From Father Abbot Peter Abelard."

His eyes lighted as he studied the top page. "It says, 'Letter to a Friend.'" Softly, he asked, "Does he mean me?"

I nodded.

After glancing quickly at the greeting, he began to read, murmuring the lines aloud, "'Often the hearts of men and women are comforted in their sorrows by example more than by words. And because you have always been a friend to me when I needed a friend, even though we are apart now, I'm sending you this history of the sufferings which have sprung out of my misfortunes. I do this so that when you compare your sorrows to mine, you may discover that yours are nothing, or at the most of small matter, and you will be able to bear them more easily.'"

Marcel's eyes glistened with tears—I saw them when he glanced up at me to say, "Spider, you need something to eat and a chance to wash away the dust of the road. I'd like to be alone for a while to read this."

I was glad to escape so that I could find Joie and Flore. I went straight to the kitchen house, where they lived now, not just during the day but at night, too.

"Aran!" Joie squealed when she saw me. "You're home!"

"Yes, I'm home." I picked her up and swung her around. "And how is my Joie?"

"Like my name. Full of joy! Because Aran has come back."

"Give him some peace for a moment, child," Flore chided in her deep voice. "Aran, I must have known you were coming, because look at what I've baked. Your favorite blue-plum tart. Dear boy, we're so glad to have you home."

Settling myself on a bench, I asked around a mouthful of the tart, "What's been happening on the estate while I was gone?"

The happiness faded from Flore's face. Frowning, she said, "You might as well hear it from me. Your scheme—about selling the yarn in Paris—it ended in disaster."

I could feel my mouth go dry around the crumbs of the tart. "Tell me."

"Well, you weren't here, so Lord Marcel sent one of his overseers to Paris with the yarn. The man returned with much less money than you said we should expect." She paused. "Joie, can you run outside and bring me two handfuls of mint leaves? They're the dark green ones that smell so good. They grow along the border under the apricot tree."

With Joie out of hearing, Flore continued softly, "The peasants began to quarrel about how much each of them was entitled to. First the women who'd actually given up their yarn squabbled among themselves. Then their husbands got drawn into it. Fights broke out. One day, out in the field where they were cutting hay, two of the men—Vincent and Arnaud—quarreled worse than ever. Arnaud swung his scythe and cut a great gash in Vincent's arm."

Remembering it, Flore squeezed her eyes shut and shuddered. I tried to swallow, but my throat felt clogged.

Flore went on, pausing often to catch her breath, "Soon after, the arm turned all red and ugly, swollen up from poisoning of the blood. We thought Vincent was sure to die, but then I remembered some herbs that are good for leaching out the poison. Two of the men carried me in my chair alongside the river until I found the right herbs. I made a poultice that spared Vincent's life, but his arm will never heal. It's useless now. The muscle was sliced to the bone."

She shook her head. "Vincent can no longer do fieldwork. His son, Marc, who's only five years old, has started to work in his father's place in the fields so the family won't starve."

As Joie returned, her small hands trailing mint leaves, Flore whispered, "She keeps asking where Marc has gone. He was her favorite playmate."

Throughout Flore's telling of the story, I'd been filled with a horror that grew and grew until I felt sick with it. All those terrible things had happened because of me, because of my misbegotten scheme to bring money to the peasants. Lord Marcel had warned me that I didn't understand how peasants think, but I hadn't believed him. And now—a man's life had been ruined. His family might starve. I wanted to run straight to the fields to dig and plow and harvest, to make up for Vincent's lost work.

Flore seized my arm. "Don't look that way, Aran. It wasn't your fault. If *you'd* sold the yarn in Paris, you'd have done it right and the peasants wouldn't have had to fight over the money. But Peter Abelard spoiled everything because he sent for you, and that left no one who knew the right way to go about those things."

"What happened to Arnaud?" I asked, low.

"Nothing much. He was given thirty lashes with a rope whip. It ripped up his back pretty bad, but I gave him what was left of the poultice. He won't scar too much."

One of the kitchen wenches came then to tell me that Lord Marcel was waiting for me. I hadn't washed off the dust of the road, but I went to him anyway, still dazed over hearing how Vincent had been sliced to the bone by Arnaud.

Marcel looked as if he hadn't moved since Abelard's manuscript reached his hands. "You should read this, Spider," he told me excitedly. "Master Abelard has written the whole story of his life, right up to this time. He calls it *Historia Calamitatum.* The Story of My Misfortunes."

Marcel pushed the pages toward me, asking, "Do you know why he sent me this letter, Spider? He wanted to write, in his own words, in his own defense, about all the—uh—regretful—things that have happened to him up till now. Partly an apology, partly an attack against his enemies. For instance, take a look at these lines: 'The more widely my fame spread and continued to grow, the more bitter was the envy those men felt against me.'"

Marcel shook his head in sympathy. "And here, look at this part where he got into trouble at the Abbey of Saint-Denis, simply because he said the real Saint Denis wasn't the founder of the abbey. Listen to this, Spider. He writes:

> 'The abbot heard the monks' story against me with delight, rejoicing at having found a chance to crush me, for the greater vileness of his life made him fear me. . . . In vain did I offer to submit to discipline if I had in any way been guilty. In utter despair at the apparent conspiracy of the whole world against me, I fled secretly from the monastery at night.'"

Marcel sighed. "Poor Abelard! How hard it was for him."

Hard for Abelard! Who'd suffered because he was continually getting into arguments with his religious superiors—this time a silly quarrel over which saint had founded an abbey; other times over the meaning of words used in theological texts. Who cared? "What about your serf, Vincent," I wanted to cry out to Marcel. "Vincent, who can no longer cut hay or cut wood because his arm is crippled, who has to send his small son to work in the fields so the family won't starve. And they'll probably starve anyway, when winter comes. That's what 'misfortune' means to the peasants on your estate!"

But I clamped my teeth shut and said nothing, not wanting Marcel to know that Flore had told me the whole sordid story. Perhaps Marcel would think to mention it to me, sooner or later. For now he was all absorbed in the letter he'd received from his hero, the famous Abelard.

Marcel leaned back in his chair and said, "Master Abelard wants me to have copies made of this letter, and he wants you to deliver them to certain churchmen he's named here."

"He does?" I straightened in surprise. When Abelard said I was to be his messenger, I thought he only meant for me to carry the one letter to Marcel. He hadn't mentioned anything to me about taking copies to different people in different places.

"It will require some time," Marcel continued. "First I'll have to send to Paris to hire a scribe. Or maybe two scribes. Even the best of them will need weeks to make good copies—this letter covers more than twenty closely written pages. The copies must be accurate and complete. Master Abelard insists on that. You know how particular he is about words."

Within a few days the scribes arrived. They set about the long and arduous task of copying Abelard's letter. Since I couldn't be of any help to them, I spent all of my free time in the kitchen house.

I was torn between wanting to work in the fields to take Vincent's place, and staying close to Flore, who was having more trouble breathing of late. When she moved suddenly, she would gasp, and often her lips and tongue and fingertips looked blue.

"It's my strength of will that keeps me alive, Aran. For Joie's sake," she told me. "How much longer I can last, I just don't know."

One day, after she'd had a particularly hard time drawing breath, she gestured for me to sit beside her. "If I die," she said, "I want you to take care of Joie. To be her guardian. Protect her."

"I will, Flore," I promised, "but she's such a little thing, she needs her mother. So you can't die." I pulled my bench even closer to her, as if I could share some of my own breath with her.

"You see how beautiful she is," Flore said.

"Yes. Everyone sees that."

"In ten more years, men will try to take her by force. You must not let that happen."

"How can I protect her?" I asked. "Do you mean you want me to marry her?"

"Oh, no," she answered quickly. "You'll never marry." She said it with such conviction that I was startled.

"What do you mean?" I asked.

Flore turned away from me and didn't answer.

"Flore?" I grasped her thin arm. "Why did you say that just now?"

Finally, with her eyes lowered, she answered me. But it was with a question. "How old are you now, Aran?"

"Seventeen."

"Do you ever look at any of the girls who work in the kitchen? They look at you. All the time." Flore pointed toward the hearth, where a couple of the kitchen wenches were giggling and glancing my way as they turned the meat on the spit.

"Many of these girls would be happy if you wooed them, Aran. You're quite handsome, you know. You have that thick mop of black hair, and a face as smooth as a baby's." Lowering her voice, she said, "Too smooth."

Self-consciously, I rubbed my cheeks with my knuckles.

"For a while," she went on, "I watched closely to see whether, since you had no interest in girls, you might like boys. But you don't."

I whispered, "What are you trying to tell me?"

To buy time so she could summon her courage, Flore called out, "Marguerite, that soup is going to get singed if you don't stir it more. But first help Spider carry my chair outside. I need a breath of fresh air."

After we'd settled her chair beneath the apricot tree, and after Marguerite had gone back to her cooking,

Flore said, "I saw what happened to you when they welded that metal shell onto you five years ago. The chains were fastened across your shoulders and between your legs. Those links were melting hot. They burned you. Badly."

"Go on."

"Your voice hasn't deepened, Aran. You have no beard. Your shoulders are narrow. Girls don't excite you. Can't you understand? That terrible heat damaged you." She breathed heavily, either from emotion or because her weak lungs made it hard to go on. "Even back then, when I saw how badly burned you were, I suspected you might be blighted for life. Remember, I was the one who took care of you all those weeks afterward. And ever since I came here, I've been watching you to notice whether—"

I leaped up. "You're wrong. I may not be brawny yet, but I'm not through growing. I'm still getting taller—by *inches* every year. And if I don't pay attention to kitchen girls"—I laughed harshly—"Well, that's easy. Don't you know why?"

She shook her head.

"I spent two years of my life with the most beautiful, the most brilliant woman on earth. Eloise! How could any other woman catch my interest, after Eloise? If I came close to her today, I'd have all the feelings men have for women, you can be sure of that, Flore. If I never marry, it's because I can't have her, and no other woman measures up—not even by the smallest whit—to Eloise."

Flore's lips pressed together in a smile that looked as though it might melt, at any moment, into weeping. "No doubt you're right," she said.

CHAPTER NINETEEN

AFTER A FEW WEEKS, LORD MARCEL CALLED ME to his chamber, where the copying was being done.

"One of these copies is finished," he told me. "Abelard wanted the first one to go to Abbot Suger at Saint-Denis Abbey, but—I've been thinking."

He perched on a chair, his hands with their heavy gold rings dangling between his knees. In a rush, he said, "The second copy is nearly completed, too, and that one can go to Abbot Suger. It's my opinion that—" Again he paused. "I really believe you should take the first copy to Eloise at the Paraclete."

My breath caught. "Eloise? At the Paraclete? Isn't that where—"

"It's the place in the wilderness where Abelard spent some time before he went to Saint-Gildas. The students built him a chapel and an oratory there, and

since then, other buildings have been added."
Standing and beginning to pace, Marcel went on,
"After Abelard left the Paraclete, Abbot Suger of
Saint-Denis decided to take back Argenteuil, where
Eloise was living as a nun. Since she and her religious
sisters had no other place to go, Abelard deeded them
the Paraclete. That's where she is now."

My heart began to beat a little faster. "And you
want me to take her a copy of this letter?"

"Don't you think that's the right thing to do?" he
asked me. "You've read the letter. You know what's in
it. Abelard has written so much about Eloise, about
how they fell in love and how she didn't want to marry
him—it seems only right to me that she ought to see
how she's portrayed, before some fat, pious old clergy-
man starts panting over the pages." Marcel shifted
through the parchments until he found the one he
wanted.

"Listen to this, Spider; I'm reading it again exactly
as Abelard has written it: 'In our desire for one
another, nothing about love was left untried. If there
was anything about lovemaking we didn't know, we
soon discovered it. Since inexperience made us all the
more passionate, our thirst for one another was never
quenched.'"

My fingers curled into fists, but Marcel didn't
notice my disquiet. "There's a lot more like that," he
said. "If this—uh—vivid description—is going to be
spread all over France, and it will be, because the

copies will be copied and copied again—then I think Eloise should know about it. Don't you agree?"

I could only nod.

"So take this first copy to the Paraclete," Marcel told me. "And when you see Mistress Eloise—I mean, Mother Abbess Eloise; even though she's young, they made her prioress because she's so highly educated—when you see her, tell her for me . . . well, maybe you'd better not say anything at all until after she reads this. I don't know how she'll feel about it."

The very same day, I saddled Charlemagne and left. How much easier it was to find places now that I could ask directions out loud. By the second day I drew near to the Paraclete, becoming more and more anxious, with each clop of Charlemagne's hooves, about meeting Eloise. Abbess Eloise. Mother Superior to a convent full of Benedictine sisters. I'd have to get used to thinking of her that way.

After I tied Charlemagne to a post set in the middle of a grassy knoll where he could graze, I rang the bell at the convent gate and waited. The gate was opened by a plump, ruddy-faced sister drying her hands on her apron.

"I have a message to deliver to Mother Abbess Eloise," I told her.

"She's at prayers in the chapel," the nun answered. "If you wait in the refectory until vespers is over, I'll tell her you're there."

She left then, and I wandered around trying to

find the refectory. Unsure which building it was, I entered a small stone room with a steeply gabled roof. Inside, it was dim and cool. Tired from my journey, I curled up in the corner farthest away from a dark wooden crucifix where only one small candle burned.

The flame cast eerie shadows on the carved body of Christ, a dying Christ with pierced hands and feet and a wounded side. Blood spattered the face beneath the crown of thorns. And the eyes—those sorrowful eyes—they gazed at me with pity and reproach over all the lies I'd told. To escape, I closed my own eyes and fell asleep.

"Bless me, Father."

Voices woke me. Near the crucifix, Eloise was kneeling in front of a priest, saying her confession.

I couldn't interrupt; I was too embarrassed to let them know I was there, intruding on what should have been a private matter. I pulled my knees close to my chest and hoped they wouldn't see me huddled in the shadows. Holding my hands over my ears, I tried not to hear, but her voice was strong.

"I can't help it, Father, the pleasures I shared with him were too sweet. I can't banish them from my thoughts."

"You must try harder, my daughter."

"I can't. Even in sleep I have no peace. I twist and turn and—and often at Mass, when I should be praying, instead I'm longing for his love—"

"Eloise!"

"It isn't fair! When he sent me to the convent he told me I should pray and offer my sufferings to God, but he doesn't suffer like I do. What my uncle did to Abelard cured him of any carnal desire, yet I'm the same woman I was before."

"Everything that happens is God's will," the priest said with patience.

Eloise interrupted hotly, "It wasn't God who mutilated Abelard! It was two horrible, demented men."

"I cannot give you absolution if you won't regret your sins," the priest told her.

"My sins! I regret all my sins, Father, but loving Abelard was never one of them. I'll never regret that."

The priest drew back from her. "You are a nun. You are an abbess. You must give up these longings of the flesh!"

"Give them up!" She laughed bitterly as her voice became harsh. "I've given up everything else, including my own son. I'm here in this convent only because Abelard told me to stay. Give up desire? With every breath I take, with every drop of blood—"

"Mother Abbess Eloise!" the priest thundered. "You dishonor your religious vocation!"

"I have no vocation!" she cried shrilly. "I never have had!" Collapsing onto the floor, she began to sob. "Do you realize, Father, that I'm only twenty-three! Twenty-three, and I've lost everything—my husband, my son, all the learning I could have had if I'd stayed in the world—"

I hoped it would soon be over; I was trembling so hard I thought they could hear my bones shake.

The priest took pity on her desolate weeping and gave her absolution before he left, but Eloise stayed there a long time, until at last her sobbing subsided. Wearily she stood, smoothed the skirt of her long black habit, and left the room, heading, no doubt, for the refectory, where I was supposed to be waiting.

Dusk had fallen. I followed Eloise, taking care to keep my footsteps so quiet that she wouldn't know I was behind her. She pushed through a heavy wooden door to the real refectory—I'd mistakenly been waiting for her in the wrong chapel. I stayed outside for a few moments, giving her time to get her emotions under control, and then I went in.

"Yes, who is it?" she asked.

Taking a candle from a sconce on the wall, I held it in front of my face.

"Spider?" she cried. "Is it you? You're so much taller! I'm overjoyed to see you. Look at you! I can't believe it—come sit down next to me and tell me all—oh, for a moment I forgot. You can't talk."

"What would you like to know?" I asked her.

For the first time, I got the reaction I'd always hoped for. She fairly leaped backward from where she stood, her eyes widening and her face lighting with excitement. "You're speaking!"

I nodded.

"How did—? When did it—?"

For one long, delicious moment I stayed silent, enjoying her amazed delight. Then I murmured, "Everyone says it was a miracle."

She took the candle from my hand and held it close to my eyes as she peered into them. "Everyone?" she asked. "What about you? What do you say it was?"

I breathed deeply . . . with relief. At last I was going to be able to shed the lie. "On the night Abelard was mutilated by your uncle Fulbert," I told her, "I stayed at the bottom of the stairs. I was supposed to be standing guard, but Fulbert and his man took me by surprise and tied my hands and legs. I couldn't free myself until they were gone, and then I ran upstairs. Master Abelard was bleeding badly. He was nearly out of his head from pain."

"And then?" she asked softly.

"He took his knife and cut my tongue, or rather, the cord of flesh that bound my tongue to the floor of my mouth." There! At last *someone* knew the truth.

"After that you could talk?"

"Not right away. It was months before I could say the first words. I still don't talk as well as other people."

"You sound wonderful to me." She came forward to embrace me. "I thought you were always going to be so small," she said, with her lips against my hair, "but now you're nearly as tall as I am."

I closed my eyes and breathed deeply of the

smell of her, of roses and wild thyme. "My name is Aran," I whispered to her, savoring the moment. "I always wanted to tell you that."

Leaning away from me, she asked, "Has Abelard learned that you can talk?"

"I tried to tell him. But even when he heard my voice, he never thought to ask how I got it back. He'd forgotten all about cutting my tongue loose."

She laughed a little. "Abelard is always so caught up in his own calamities that he never notices the drama in anyone else's life. That's why I was good for him. I *made* him see things."

The word "calamities" reminded me of why I had come. *Historia Calamitatum.* "What's this?" she asked after I reached inside my tunic and handed her the rolled-up manuscript. Glancing at the top page, which was a note from Marcel, she turned pale.

"Come with me," she said quietly.

She filled my hands with unlighted candles and led me to a table where we lit them, one by one, from the candle I'd been holding. "Sit here," she said, gesturing to a bench. As she unrolled the pages on the table, I leaned across and helped her straighten their curled edges.

While she read, I studied her. She'd changed, if in no other way than by having her hair completely hidden under the white wimple around her face. It made her look too mature. Before, she'd seemed girlish; now all trace of that was gone. The black veil over the wimple, and the long black habit she wore, lent her a somberness that was not becoming.

Once she realized the main body of the letter was from Abelard, I might as well not have been there at all. She grew entirely absorbed in it until she finished reading the whole thing. When she looked up at me then, I was surprised to see an expression I hadn't expected in her eyes. Anger!

"So he calls this 'A Letter to a Friend,' does he? It would have been nice if he'd written a letter to his wife! Not once since I became a nun have I received from him as much as a line scrawled on a discarded bit of parchment."

At times, being speechless is a useful escape. Before, she wouldn't have expected me to answer; now I was supposed to say something, and I didn't know what it should be.

"Aran, I hope you can wait here for a day or two, because I want to write a reply to Abelard," she declared. "Can you stay?"

I considered. I knew I was supposed to hurry back to Lord Marcel to pick up the next copy of *Historia Calamitatum* and deliver it to Abbot Suger; Abelard had insisted that I was the only person allowed to carry the letters. Because everyone knew I was his servant, he'd written, the copies were to be given out by my hands and mine alone, so no one could doubt that *Historia Calamitatum* was authentic.

But what difference would a day or two make?

For that small space of time, I could change my plans. If Eloise wanted to write to her neglectful lord and master, her husband, and her religious superior—and all of them were the same man—then I would wait.

During those two days of waiting, I tramped through the fields of the Paraclete, imagining what it must have been like when Abelard lived there surrounded by droves of students who kept coming and coming. Most of the makeshift huts they'd built had fallen into ruin; the thatch roofs were rotted from neglect, and the clay that plastered the outsides had dissolved in heavy rains. Before long, no one would ever know that all those crude little hives had once dotted the wild landscape.

The main chapel of the Paraclete was still strong, though, and would probably last a hundred years or more. There'd been a death since the nuns had moved in—one of the sisters had died of old age. Villagers had dug out a crypt beneath the chapel, where the old nun's body now lay interred.

The stone crypt was private and silent. When I found it, I sat there to think, leaning against the wall.

Not a single hour had passed since Flore had said that terrible thing she'd said about me that I hadn't worried over it, thrashed it around inside my head, doubted Flore, doubted myself, and wondered if it could possibly be true. My mind would never be at peace until I'd proven it to myself one way or another.

The nuns sang compline in the oratory at nine

o'clock at night, and then they all went to bed. Apologizing, Eloise had told me I was not allowed to sleep inside the convent because I was a—she'd hesitated, trying to decide whether to say "boy" or "man." Which was what I wanted to find out, too.

The nuns had fixed a comfortable bed for me inside the barn, where I'd slept the past two nights, close to Charlemagne's stall. But this would be my last night at the Paraclete. I needed to act soon if I were ever going to lay my doubts to rest.

After dark, I found it easy enough to slip out of the barn and steal into the convent building. No precautions had been taken to keep me out—probably because Mother Abbess Eloise trusted me, and anyway, I appeared harmless enough. I found her room; it was no more than a small cell, even though she was the religious superior. Dim light coming from beneath the door let me guess she was still working on her reply to Abelard, writing by the flame of a candle. The letter had taken days to write because the nuns' hours were constantly interrupted by calls to prayer.

After a very long time, the light went out. I waited, sitting on the floor opposite her door, my head against the timbered wall. When I thought she must finally be asleep, I got up.

Stealthily, I unlatched her door. It was easy—I just inserted a thin stick into the hole the iron latch went through, and gently lifted it. The door hinges didn't squeak because earlier, while the nuns had

been singing their evening service, I'd taken the pre-
caution of greasing those hinges.

I crept across the room to where she lay asleep.
She wore only a shift. Her short-cropped hair curled
damply around her face. Without a wimple hiding her
cheeks and hair, she looked so much younger, like the
Eloise I'd first seen in Paris, when she was hardly
more than my age now.

The room had only a narrow slit in the wall to
serve as a window. It let in the outside air, and also a
thin shaft of moonlight that illuminated both of us as
I bent over her.

My face was only inches above hers. I could see
the dewy trace of perspiration on her upper lip. I
leaned even closer, until her breath felt soft against
my lips. As she sighed deeply in her sleep, the neck of
her shift fell open and I saw her breasts. How beautiful! So beautiful—!

Yes. Lovely beyond what a man could endure.
And I felt nothing. Nothing at all.

Silently and swiftly I backed out of the patch of
moonlight and into the dark shadows near the wall.
Slipping out of the room and carefully latching the
door behind me, I fought hard to hold back my sobs
until I reached the safety of the barn. There I threw
myself against Charlemagne's neck and wept bitterly
through half the night.

What was I? Not a man, that was certain.

What was I good for? Nothing!

I'd wanted to be able to speak, foolishly thinking I could be an orator like Abelard. Instead, I was a eunuch like Abelard. But Abelard had been a full-grown man before he was castrated, so his voice would always stay rich and deep, while I—who hadn't been castrated, but was damaged with the same results—would always sound treble, like a woman.

Even if I'd had a voice as powerful as Abelard's, I thought scornfully to myself, I had nothing worthwhile to say with it. The smattering of learning I'd gained from listening to Abelard's lectures made me fit for nothing! Although I could read, I couldn't even write my own name.

Celibate! What good was it to be celibate unless I became a monk? I thought about those villainous monks at Saint-Gildas and I shuddered. I thought about those vindictive priests who'd made Abelard burn his book at Soissons and I cursed. Even though there were other, decent men in religious orders, celibacy had no value as an offering to God unless it was *chosen*, not thrust upon a person. And I was like Eloise—*I had no vocation!* Without a vocation, Eloise had gone into a nunnery anyway. And she was miserable.

Help others? I'd failed at that, too. After I'd convinced Lord Marcel to sell the yarn in Paris, Vincent had been cut and crippled. Even the smoke holes were useless—once the cool autumn rains began, the women refused to open the trapdoors because they said heat from the fires escaped with the smoke, and the rain came in through the hole overhead. My great ideas had turned into laughable blunders.

What kind of man would I ever be? Any kind at all? I could never make love to a woman, never father a child. I was as neuter as a docked lamb, but even a lamb has some purpose. It gives wool or, at the least, ends up on some family's dinner plates.

What was I good for!

When the pale gray dawn of autumn seeped through the cracks under the barn door, I crawled off the cold floor and went outside to the well. The nuns were already at Prime in the chapel. I could hear their high, sweet voices singing the divine office. Again and again I splashed cold water on my face, trying to wash away the signs of my tortured night.

Not long after, one of the nuns brought me breakfast and said, "Mother Abbess Eloise says she'll see you in the courtyard after Terce." Terce was another session of prayer. Benedictine nuns, as well as monks, prayed together many times a day.

When Eloise arrived she told me, "Last night I finished writing my letter to Abelard." If she noticed how wretched and exhausted I looked, she didn't mention it. "But there's one more matter I need to settle with you, Aran. Wait here."

She went back into the convent building. Had I carelessly left any sign behind me last night, evidence that I'd entered her room? Was that what she was going for? My hands began to sweat.

Quickly enough, Eloise returned, holding something behind her back. "I have a gift for you," she said. "Do you remember this?" She held it out to me.

It was the brown cloak we'd woven together at Le Pallet.

"It's no longer useful to me," she said. "Now I have to wear this ugly black habit all the time. I should have given this cloak to the poor, but there are so many memories woven into it. . . . Anyway, I want you to have it, Aran." She shook out the folds and held it up against me. "You've grown a lot since we wove this, so you need to make it longer, but you can do that. You're so good at spinning and weaving."

Inside, I writhed. When I died, was that what they'd say over my grave? "He was so good at spinning and weaving." What an epitaph for a man!

"I suppose you must go now," she said. "And I have to get back to my duties."

In Charlemagne's left saddlebag I put the letter for Abelard, and in the right one I put the big round loaf of bread Eloise gave me. "As nuns, we're supposed to feed and clothe the poor," she said, smiling, "so I've given you bread and a warm cloak. But you don't look poor at all, Aran. You look quite prosperous now. I'm glad Marcel is looking out for you. And I'll give you my blessing, for whatever it's worth, so that God will look after you, too."

I nodded.

"I haven't heard your voice this morning, Aran.

You're as silent as you used to be. Is anything wrong?"

"Nothing's wrong," I said, turning my eyes away. "Thank you for the cloak and the food."

When I stopped at the road to wave back toward her, she shouted, "Take the letter to Abelard right away, will you?"

Feeling miserable, I kicked Charlemagne into a trot. When we reached the main road, I pulled on his reins to halt him while I made up my mind what to do.

I'd already lost two days. Marcel had told me to deliver the copy of Abelard's letter to Eloise, and then come straight back so I could carry the second copy to Abbot Suger. I'd thought that after that, I would take Eloise's letter to Abelard.

But she wanted me to deliver it right away. If I went to Saint-Gildas first, it would delay me by at least ten extra days before I could return to Marcel at Rambouillet. I felt pulled in two directions, but I decided to do what Eloise wanted. "What does it matter? What does *anything* matter?" I cried out, feeling so sorry for myself that I didn't care which direction I took. Ever. I dug my heels into Charlemagne and turned onto the road that headed for Saint-Gildas.

The sun was bright as I rode through the forest. Curiosity tugged at me. More than anything, I wanted to know what Eloise had written to Abelard. Twisting in my saddle, I opened the flap of the saddlebag and pulled out her letter. She hadn't sealed it.

I lifted one corner of the parchment, just enough to see a few of the lines. She seemed to be scolding him with the same words I'd heard her speak: that if he were going to write to anyone, it should have been to her. Then, once I began, I couldn't stop reading.

The path through the forest was deserted. Because I was all alone, I decided to read the letter aloud, hoping that if I shouted hard enough, some of the pain inside me might ride on the words and escape into the trees. My voice might be high, but it was also very loud.

Those words! At first I almost sang them out: "'You know, my beloved—and the whole world knows—how much I have lost in losing you. How one wretched stroke of treachery robbed me of my whole existence, by robbing me of you.'"

I had to stop shouting; what she'd written was too moving. In a softer voice I continued: "'I carried out all your commands, even though it nearly destroyed me. My love rose to such heights of madness that I lost everything I most desire when I did your bidding, and put on this black habit I now wear—to prove that you, and you alone, possess both my body and my will. God knows I never wanted anything from you except yourself. I wanted no marriage bond. It was not my own pleasure and wishes, ever, that I yearned to gratify, but yours.'"

Now my voice dropped to a whisper. "'The name

of wife may seem more sacred to some, but to me, the name of mistress, whenever I remember what I once was to you, will always sound sweeter.'"

I couldn't read it aloud any longer because I choked over the heartbreak in her words.

After I finished the whole letter, reading silently, I brought Charlemagne to a halt again. We'd reached a small clearing.

How beautiful the day was. A breeze lifted the leaves on their branches and carried the smell of wild thyme and asters. Above, the sky softened as the sun moved past its zenith, making tree patterns all around me. Behind me lay the Paraclete, where Eloise remained imprisoned in the shadow and silence of those stone walls. Now I knew, without any doubt, that she hadn't wanted to take the veil—not at all. She'd professed her vows as a nun and entered the convent because that was what Abelard had told her to do. *After* he could no longer be her lover.

Loss! How much we'd lost, all of us.

And yet—not everything was meaningless and empty. Abelard had been gelded, yes, but he still possessed the keenest mind in Europe. Eloise still had her son. Even though she'd given him up, he was thriving, she'd told me, under the care of Denise and Hugh, and surely, one day, she'd see him again.

I'd lost the power to ever father a child of my own, but I had Joie, who thought the sun rose and set on me. True, I'd had a father who'd beat me and a brother who'd sold me, yet I'd also had a kind and gentle mother who'd loved me more than anything in her life.

And I had something else. Right at that moment, clutched in my hands, I had the words of Eloise.

Charlemagne lowered his head to graze. Still I sat, unmoving in my saddle, thinking. If I took that letter to Abelard, he would read it impatiently and put it aside, because he was wholly occupied with trying to control his unruly monks and with trying to win sympathy for himself from scholars. Sooner or later Eloise's letter would be lost, through Abelard's carelessness. Or maybe his monks would steal the letter so they could sell the sheepskin parchment to someone else, who would then rub off Eloise's words with a rough stone, and write new words where hers had been.

Or . . . I could turn around and ride back to Marcel DuChesne. Show him Eloise's letter. Let him make copies. As Marcel said, all copies beget other copies, which beget still more copies. And only after that would I take the original to Abelard.

Abelard's letters would live forever, because he'd made sure they'd be copied and read by a dozen scholars and churchmen who would pass them along to still others. The story of Abelard and Eloise would always be known through his eyes.

But Eloise's words would disappear from the world. Unless . . . I chose to save them.

I could make them survive. *I* was the one who had the power to let the story be told as Eloise saw it—through the hot tears of the incomparable woman I'd always loved but could never love.

If the words Abelard wrote were eagles that soared, then the words Eloise wrote were falcons. They dove right into the heart. They deserved to be read by everyone.

It was up to me. My decision. I smiled. So there *was*, after all, something I could do that was worthwhile.

To Saint-Gildas, or to Rambouillet?

I chose Rambouillet.

CHAPTER TWENTY

By choosing Rambouillet I began to spin the web that bound Abelard and Eloise to each other over the years to come. More than that, my web spread outward, touching countless others who have read the letters, and by reading them, have felt their own hearts entangled in this story of desperate love.

I won't say I became a skilled horseman during my travels, but Charlemagne and I got used to each other's ways, and grew fond of one another. Since I spent more time with Charlemagne than with any other warm-blooded creature in my life, I took good care of him.

In my hooded brown cloak, I blended with Charlemagne's sorrel coat so completely that we looked like one single—and rather drab—creation. Maybe that's why no one paid much attention to us.

Days and weeks, months and seasons, went by. Eloise stayed quietly in her convent, tending to her duties and her nuns. Abelard finally fled from Saint-Gildas after he discovered his monks were plotting against him once again—this time to slit his throat! He moved from place to place, always adored by his students, always hounded by his enemies.

And always getting into trouble. He'd begun to lecture again, and he once told a classroom full of students, "A doctrine should not be believed only because God said it, but because we can convince ourselves by our own reasoning that it is true."

Heresy! the churchmen cried. The uproar was deafening—not from the students, who enjoyed being told that they should think for themselves, but from Abelard's religious superiors. He was forced to write more treatises to defend himself.

Arguments and letters weren't the only things that came pouring from Abelard's pen. He began to compose music, too, for the religious services at the Paraclete. "Take this to Mother Abbess Eloise," he told me one raw day in March. "I know you just returned from Laon, but you're young and you don't need much rest between journeys. I want you to get this music to them by the beginning of Holy Week so the nuns have time to rehearse it for Easter."

Disappointed, because I wanted to spend Easter with Flore and Joie, I nevertheless obeyed him, as I always did. The weather was blustery, with storms and sleet following me all the way to the Paraclete. Even the tightly woven brown cloak couldn't keep me dry.

The leather of Charlemagne's saddlebags had been well sealed against the elements, so the manuscript arrived at the Paraclete no worse for wear. Since Mother Abbess Eloise was in bed with a cold, the nuns made me welcome, and took Abelard's music into their hands.

It was called an *Epithalamica*, a liturgical sequence meant especially for Easter Day. The nuns hurried to the oratory to practice it.

"It's the Bible story of the wise and foolish virgins and the coming of the bridegroom," one of the nuns told me later that day. "Of course, the bridegroom is meant to be Jesus Christ. Since Mother Eloise is confined to her bed with illness, we've had a chance to try out the music in secret. It's lovely! We're going to surprise her with it on Easter Day."

They practiced long hours during the remainder of Holy Week. On Holy Saturday Eloise was feeling a little better and was able to join her nuns for supper for their first breaking of the Lenten fast. But they wouldn't let her hear the new music. They buzzed among themselves, smiling with anticipation over the treat they were saving for her.

Since I wasn't allowed inside the convent, I took my meals alone in the refectory. On that Saturday, after supper, I stood outside Eloise's cell and called to her through the narrow slit of the window.

"Mother Abbess Eloise, it's Aran. Can you come to the window?"

When she reached it she said, whispering because her throat was raw, "They told me you were here. You've seen Abelard, then?"

"I just came from him."

"How is he?"

"Aching from that fall from his horse. Even though it happened months ago, he can't seem to get rid of the soreness."

"And is he as imperious as ever?" she asked. Although I could barely see her, I could hear the amusement in her voice.

I smiled, too. "Maybe more than ever. But . . . I need to speak to you about another matter, Mother Abbess Eloise."

"Oh, for God's sake, Aran, after all we've been through together, you can call me Eloise."

"Yes. Eloise. It's about Joie. I've told you her mother wants me to be her guardian."

Eloise coughed hard, and when she recovered, asked, "How old is the child now, Aran? Seven? That's the same age as my son Astrolabe." Wistfully, she said, "How I wish I could see him." After a deep sigh that caused her to cough again, she went on, "What is it you want to ask me about Joie?"

It was hard for me to tell her what I dreaded so much, but what I couldn't escape preparing for. "Flore is dying. She won't last long. She can't even sit up anymore. And I travel all the time, so after Flore's gone, I won't be able to take care of Joie—"

"You want to bring her here to the Paraclete. You want the nuns to raise her."

"No." I shook my head. "I want *you* to raise her. To educate her. She's really bright—I've already taught her to read some, but I want her to learn to write, too, and I can't teach her because I don't know how myself. And Lady Clarisse won't allow Lord Marcel to have Joie tutored because she says the child is just a servant with no known father."

"Hmmmm." Eloise frowned at that. "Marcel's wife, Lady Clarisse—has she conceived yet?"

"No. They're still childless."

"Then it's no wonder she doesn't want Marcel taking an interest in someone else's child. Of course you can bring Joie here, Aran. If she's as bright as you say, it will give me joy to teach her." She laughed a little. "Joy. Her name portends a happy life for her."

She coughed again, felt a chill, and had to lie down. No one knew whether Mother Abbess Eloise would be strong enough to attend the long Easter service the next day.

But she came. On Easter morning, still feeling weak, she entered the oratory. Instead of standing in front near the altar, Eloise stayed in the back, leaning against the wall, close to the door so she could escape if her coughing started up again too harshly. I took my place next to her as the Mass began.

Sound has always been able to transfix me, from Abelard's powerful orations to the love songs the students sang in the taverns. But this! I'd never heard anything as beautiful as those high, pure voices of the nuns, echoing off the stone walls of the oratory as they sang the music Abelard wrote, inspired by the Song of Songs:

> "'Young maidens, sing! Dance!
> When the bride begins her song, join in!
> The bridegroom's friends have called you to
>   the wedding.
> See? The bridegroom comes leaping upon the
>   mountains, comes racing over the hills. . . .
> He says, "Arise, my love, make haste!
> "My snow-white dove, come fly with me!"'"

Eloise had turned deathly pale, and I knew it wasn't because she'd been ill. The singing of the nuns was enough to pierce anyone's heart.

> "'Grief has brought me a sleepless night,
> My grief, made unendurable by my love,
> But my desire grows even stronger from
>   this delay,
> Until my lover comes to his beloved.'"

Her fingers dug into the mortar between the stone blocks. She didn't weep. Not then.

> "'This is the day that has brought us
> laughter. . . .
> This is the day that arouses the bridegroom,
> This is the day that awakens the bride,
> This is the day that restores all things,
> This is the day, the loveliness of spring,
> This is the day, the world of delight. . . .'"

Eloise fainted.

Villagers from Nogent-sur-Seine had come to hear Easter Mass at the Paraclete; several of the men carried her outside into the air.

As I saw her struggling to regain consciousness, and saw her cheeks wet with tears, I thanked God for what He'd spared me. I would never have to feel the anguish of a love like Eloise and Abelard's. And I was glad. I'd seen enough of it to know how much it hurt.

Yet, even though I'd be safe from the torment, I'd miss the exultation, too. It didn't matter, I told myself. I'd already made peace with what I was.

I stayed at the Paraclete a few more days until Eloise had grown nearly well again. On my last day there, she was able to come to the refectory to talk to me.

"Bring Joie to me whenever you wish," she said. "I'll keep her here until she's old enough to be married, and then I'll help find a good husband for her. Maybe a small landowner—"

"No!" I cried. "Joie will choose for herself—she won't be forced into marriage. I plan to take her to

"No!" I cried. "Joie will choose for herself—she won't be forced into marriage. I plan to take her to Paris when she's seventeen to let her hear some of the lectures. She's so lovely that all the students will want to marry her, especially after you've educated her. She'll be like you, Eloise."

"Like me?" Eloise rested her chin on her hands and lowered her eyelids. The loose black sleeves fell back from her arms, but other, tighter black sleeves were beneath them, since a nun's habit hid everything except face and hands. "Is that what you really want, Aran—for Joie to be like me? To fall wildly in love the way I did and live a life of torment and heartbreak?"

"But you *lived!*" I said. "More than I ever will. More than anyone else has. Why do you think they still sing Abelard's songs about you in all the taverns of Paris? Why are his letters read over and over, and told aloud to the people who can't read?"

"And your letters, too," I might have added, although Eloise and I never talked about that. She had to know, though, that because of me, her words had become as famous as Abelard's.

She raised her eyes then, and asked softly, "Was it worth it, Aran? All that we did?" Taking my hand, she held it tightly.

"It was," I answered. "You know that it was."

All things to nothingness descend,
They grow old, fail, and reach the end.

Men die, iron rusts, wood turns decayed,
Towers fall, walls sink,
Sweet roses fade.

Not long does any name resound
Beyond the grave—unless it's found
Inside a book.

Only the pen
Can make immortal,
Women and men.

Wace, Anglo–Norman chronicler
1100–74

AUTHOR'S NOTE

Spider's Voice is a work of fiction, but many of the incidents in this story actually happened. Although Aran is a fictional character, Abelard and Eloise were real people who lived in the twelfth century. Their letters still exist, and have been collected by Betty Radice in the book titled *The Letters of Abelard and Heloise*, published by Viking Press. You'll notice that in the above title, "Heloise" is spelled with an "H." Since in the French language the "H" is silent, I've chosen, in this novel, to spell "Eloise" the way it's pronounced.

The full text of Abelard's *Historia Calamitatum* can be accessed on the Internet at:

http://www.fordham.edu/halsall/basis/abelard-histcal.html

Eloise's first letter to Abelard, the one Aran reads from in this novel, also can be accessed at:

http://www.fordham.edu/halsall/source/heloise1.html

A CD recording called *12th Century Chants*, subtitled *Abelard: Hymns and Sequences for Heloise*, is available from Herald AV Publications. On it, the *Epithalamica* is sung by the Schola Gregoriana of Cambridge and the Choristers of Winchester Cathedral.

Abelard died in 1142 and was buried at the

Paraclete. Eloise died in 1164 and was buried next to him. In 1817 their remains were moved to the Père Lachaise Cemetery in Paris, where today, people in love place flowers at the tomb of France's most famous lovers, Abelard and Eloise.